LOVE STORIES *in* AFRICA

BEATRICE FAIRBANKS CAYZER

ISBN:
Paperback   978-1-954341-22-7

Writers' Branding
1800-608-6550
www.writersbranding.com
orders@writersbranding.com

CONTENTS

PART ONE

CHAPTER 1

Christmas Day, 2009

My husband was murdered in Darfur three months ago. His hands were chopped off at the wrists and a machete was used to slice open his chest. Later his heart was removed, or so I've been told by the doctors from Khartoum who hinted it had been sold to traders in body parts.

Those traders have a thriving business in this region.

Only twenty-eight, a genius at cricket in his University of Newcastle days, my husband traveled to Africa immediately after graduation. He came to Darfur's refugee camps to work with people suffering from AIDS. At the same time he intended to help the children overcome their memories of horrors by offering them the joy and future financial successes that sport can provide.

He gave as examples African-American athletes: Serena Williams, for tennis, and Tiger Woods for golf. For cricket he told them about the English star, David Beckham.

His name was Lloyd Phelps. He had a superb athletic frame when I met him in Newcastle. Tall, with bright green eyes and crisp curls on his neck that I used to fondle, he was a handsome athlete. But by the time I came to Darfur to marry him, his physique had shrunk and he'd become emaciated, with sunken eyes and thinned hair.

Lloyd's last words to me as he lay bleeding away his life were: "Take care of the children.I love you…"

We'd had no children of our own. We'd been married less than two years, and had a distance-marred relationship before our wedding with no sex involved. Plenty of that later! We'd found bliss during those sublime long hours of sex in the Sudan's torrid climate. All the misery I'd seen during the daylight hours would vanish when I was in his arms and his penis entered my body. Orgasms were sublime, but produced no children.

Lloyd had been referring to our three orphans.

CHAPTER 2

Three months after Lloyd's death, on Christmas morning, while I crouched on the dirt floor of my cottage beside the orphans, singing with them AWAY IN A MANGER, to teach them a few words in English, there was little to cheer me in our cottage's one bare room.

In my window-less cottage, like prisoners in a dungeon, we heard no birds singing outside. The only sounds were cockroaches scuttling close to us and the never-ceasing wails of hungry children tolling from all over the camp.

The smells of the Christmas dinner I'd cooked were far from appetizing, we'd only some unsweetened maize boiling on the stove. The children could hardly wait to devour their dinner, whatever it was. While it was still cooking, and I had their attention, I gave them their daily English lesson.

Lloyd and I had believed that a second language would open more doors for them. Darfur's intense heat was less inside the cottage than in the dust-filled overcrowded camp. We huddled on my dirt floor, but not too close together because our body warmth made the heat worse. An infrequent puff of breeze came through the open doorway, the half-broken door still hanging on its snapped hinges from when the murderer found Lloyd here.

When I started "The cat says meow" hoping the children would copy my words as I pointed to a cat in a copybook, I was dreading their bath time knowing there wasn't enough water or soap. Their little bodies were scabbing from lack of hygiene.

"You in there," came the camp Director's surly voice, interrupting the lesson. He's a burly, bread-loaf-shaped gold-toothed black he who has been trying to invade my privacy since my arrival almost two years ago. "You, come out. No more this cottage. You go." He called.

My joints ached from crouching, but I stumbled erect to be polite and show some basic respect for the hateful Director. I strode outside to face him.

"Why? Why must I go? And where to?"

"Out! Away!"

"I'll need some place to live. Some work." I argued shrilly, and even to myself I sounded like a harpy.

"Live? Work? Your problem."

The Director slithered away like a cobra into the camp's dust. When his pudgy form disappeared into the fluctuating twilight, I packed up my children's spare belongings and my own more considerable luggage. My clothes functioned like a security blanket. I knew I wouldn't need cocktail dresses and the woolens I'd brought from Newcastle, but I was painfully nostalgic about my happy times with Lloyd when I'd worn them on our dates in college, and felt determined to keep what I could for as long as I could.

Leading my orphans into the dusty spaces between tents, we caught sight of an Ethiopian who'd recently arrived here, Malaku Galo. He had come to the camp to investigate the murder of his brother, Haile Galo.

Like a forlorn grouse left behind by his covey. Malaku Galo had begun to lose his imperious looks since arriving at the camp.Very tall, with the fine posture of plateau Amharics, he had the aquiline nose, thin lips, and caramel color of his people. But starvation was taking its toll. His shoulders slumped. What had been an attractive wooly cap of hair now had overgrown, transforming his head to look like a Sambo doll's.

"Mrs. Ella," he bowed like a French marquis to kiss my free hand. "Is this not the hour when you teach the English language? And what are these suitcases? Why do the children have their belongings with them?"

"The Director's kicked us out of my cottage."

A long, poignant moment of silence took over. I stared at Malaku, and at the three year old with him.

Malaku said: "On Christmas! You, madame, have all my sympathies."

"Thank you," I tried to smile cheerily at the little nephew.

Malaku's dirge-like voice continued as he moaned on. "I, too, have been dislodged. And with my brother's little son, Tekla. We have no place to live now in this camp."

While Malaku spoke, we watched shoals of teenage boys rush past. The Moslems brandished sticks, pretending they had spears. The Coptic Christians held high their home-made crosses of twigs, pointing them at the rival gangs as if --like shaking crosses at vampires--this would make them fade away.

"Did you know that Tekla's father, Galo, had been murdered here?"Malaku's voice grew different. His Ethiopian's bulging eyeballs — very typical of high-class Amharas from the plateaus --seem to grow ever larger. "I cannot leave this place without knowing what happened. What instigated the assassination of my brother." Malaku's use of ponderous words underlined the intensity of his feelings.

Tekla showed no emotion. He'd witnessed so much slaughter after Ethiopia's era of Red Terror.

Malaku added: "Galo had to join the Red army or be killed, so he thought he'd be cared for in Darfur where refugee camps were already set up. He make bad choice!After killed he was here, his handssliced off were. Buthis kidneys were stolen, notheart; as heard I have was the case after your husband's murder."

I had no time for listening to more sad stories. I was only concerned for the three year old Tekla and my own orphans: I didn't want them to hear this grisly information.

Meanwhile my own problem was pressing.

I turned away, thinking I could find the Director's office by following the old telegraph poles. But these had been pulled down, by refugees to hold up tents, and now the telegraph lines swung uselessly like jungle vines.

Malaku's voice flared up, like a highly active volcano."A man from London's due to arrive and there's no other accommodation for him and his three Sudanese orphans except your cottage. Man to do work of Administrator. That's heard I have."

"New arrival? Well, it must be true. Since we've been ejected out of the cottage." I pushed sweat and grimy hair from my forehead: I'd only been minutes from outside the cottage's interior and already my blonde fringe was matted to mousy brown by perspiration and the dust. "But surely that pathetic little hut can hardly be good enough for someone important. And, who's come out from London!"

"Oh, madame, I fear misinformed you I have. Your hut for new Administrator is not. He big important man. Your hut for another. This other important was. But no longer. Resigned job before left London. As volunteer comes he. Fill in for Administrator until comes big man."

"Sorry, Malaku. I don't understand. Two Administrators? But the one from London is a volunteer? That means he will be very poor."
"Volunteer not from London just: I should more specific have been. He at the Home Office worked. Big job there. But the news is that this volunteer that job left. Now, unpaid volunteer."

"Unpaid! That's the answer to why he's downgraded to such a terrible hut. I'll miss it, but it won't be good enough for a man of any importance." I took a deep breath of the smelly, windless air. "Does he get an office?"

Malaku had to pause before replying, while two more shoals of teenagers crowded this narrow lane. These were teenage girls, all with at least one baby, several with newborns and toddlers. All were Moslems, wearing green headscarves, but chatting as easily as if they were shopping on London's Oxford Street. No sticks for swords for them.

When Malaku resumed, he kept swiveling as if he was on a piano stool. He looked beyond me to check there was no eavesdropper. "Yes, Mrs. Ella, he an office has. I there precede you."

We left the trail for a wider lane. It ended at an impressive tent. "Administrator's office," Malaku said quietly, his active-volcano emotions temporarily under control. He took my free hand, and after kissing it again marquis-style, he took off with Tekla to pursue his own tragedy.

There were lights and machines rattling in the big tent although it was Christmas. I thought, "That new man 's beavering away, working on a holiday!""

A shabby leather flap covered the tent's oversized entrance. Unable to start off being polite by knocking, I took a deep breath of the tepid air and marched inside with my troupe of orphans.

Unfortunately the Administrator's temporary replacement, Ray Bruce, was dictating a letter and frowned at the interruption. I frowned in return. With both of us frowning at each other, we got off to a poor start.

"I'm Ray Bruce," he said with no welcome to me as he dismissed the secretary with a wave. "And you are?"

Staring rudely, thinking of my dear dead Lloyd's physical deterioration, I resented Ray Bruce's healthy body and glowing skin, his cared-for teeth and thick auburn hair. When he stared in return, I found my voice to burst out: "I'm Ella Phelps, the lady you took the cottage from. I want it back. I've no other place to live with these children."

"Ah, it's the cottage problem." Ray pulled at his chin as if he wore a beard. I wondered if he'd only recently shaved one off. I liked the square chin. I couldn't stop myself thinking what a good thing it was that he hadn't got a beard. I'd never liked a beard on a man. I wouldn't want to kiss a man with a beard in case there were germs trapped in the hairs. But I stopped myself from thoughts of kissing, and concentrated on my cottage.

"Yes. Cottage."

Ray Bruce continued: "I've dealt with that. The Director gave me some idea of what he was up to. Specifically, I guessed he was throwing out someone else to give me the place. So I've made arrangements to share digs with a French Medecins Sans Frontieres friend. The Director evicted you?"

"Yes, he has."

"Sorry to hear that. Not much more I can do. Dicey fellow, the Director. No doubt your cottage's going to one of his friends, now that he knows I don't want it."

"If he has any friends," I growled.

"I do have a suggestion, however. I brought three orphans with me from the last camp I visited in Darfur. I'd been to several earlier, but I wasn't permitted to bring away any children. The Administrators practically accused me of being a pedophile."

"Which camps?"

"Hamadiya, too much dust, not enough food. Touloum, ninety miles from anywhere with available food. Dereiga, tarted up for the visit of some movie star called Ambassador Mia Farrow."

"Mia Farrow! Golly. We haven't had a soul of any kind of fame here!"

"The two worst camps were Abu Sharif, and Otash. Still being attacked by government troops. So-called troops. Really nothing more than local Arabs who were promised a cut if any minerals are found in the area. The Arabs hate the Bari and the Nuba: blacks.At the next camp, where I was allowed to adopt three small boys, I did: blacks, They've been put up by Belgian nuns on the outskirts of this camp. Try those nuns. And I'll wish you luck."

I felt dismissed. This Ray Bruce hadn't been rude, but he'd been brief. Maybe he really was busy?

Trying a watery smile, I gave a brief bow and led my children outside.

I had to pause. My vulva was acting up. WHAT WAS HAPPENING TO ME? I was opening up *down there.*Oh God. I haven't even looked at another man these past three months, mourning Lloyd full time. Now this?Having these sex urges for a man who will take for HIS polio program what little funds are available for our AIDS work in Darfur? And yet I was yearning for this man I'd only seen for minutes.

What urges would I get if I'm ever with him for half an hour!My brain told me that this man was using his position for his own agenda. Why is it that my flesh calls out for him? That I want him *down there.* Entered.

CHAPTER 3

Feeling giddy, weak in the knees, I led my children away from his tent. Not far away a crowd was gathering. It was peopled by angry hungry protestors, aiming to disrupt the Interim Administrator's morning. I shrugged at their slogans and outbursts: their sufferings were my sufferings but I knew better than to try to make changes during the reign of the present Director, or while we had a temporary Administrator.

Lugging my suitcase by one hanging strap, which pulled harder at my shoulder each passing moment, I struggled to keep up with my children who were whooping with glee that they weren't having any more lessons this morning.

I knew where those Belgian nuns were located. I'd collected a bed from them when Lloyd and I first moved children into our cottage.

At that time there was a story making the rounds:it told how a ghastly crime had been committed. The body of a thirteen-year-old boy, who had been living with the nuns until puberty, had been found dismembered. After leaving the nuns the boy had nowhere to live and had ended up sharing a tent with dangerous newcomers. It turned out that these newcomers were part of a gang of body-snatchers, who had fattened him up like a Christmas goose to insure that all his organs were in great condition: then he'd been slaughtered and his organs sold.

I'd heard all the horrific details on my first visit to the nuns.

My two eldest boys were becoming unruly on the airless, dusty trail.I loved them, but had to try to tame them so as not to draw unwanted attention.

We'd reached the makeshift cemetery where my Lloyd's desecrated body had been so hastily buried that terrible day, now over three months ago. Felko, the eldest of my orphans, rejected my pleas for quiet. "This be place where husband went without heart," he hollered.

We were stared at by Moslem passersby, who knew little about this Christian cemetery. Again I attempted to shush dear but naughty Felko: "No, no. Say nothing," I urged. But I led the children into the cemetery, heavy suitcase or no.

After struggling to locate the so-called plot where Lloyd's altered remains had been planted, I dried ungovernable tears and had to plead with my orphans to come away.

It was dark when we finally reached the jumble of tents that served as the convent for my friendly Belgian nuns.

When I called gently beside the lead tent's closed flap, asking the nuns to give us hospitality, I heard some unexpected grumbling from one of the nuns. They must have retired for the night, because when a young novice called Agnes came to the flap she wasn't wearing her regulation wimple-topped headpiece.

Shy, embarrassed to be caught with hair sticking out of a makeshift head-covering, Agnes stuttered: "Reverend Mother is at her prayers." She spoke in French with a Belgian dialect, heavily accented by Flemish vowels.

Feeling shy myself, knowing I was an unwelcome intruder at such a late-for-the nuns' hour, I blushed like a schoolgirl at a porno film.

"I know you have your own problems," I said to Agnes in my halting French, "but we need beds. Here. Please!"

I recalled that this order of nuns had been made to leave Rwanda under threat of rape and death. Beds were not too much for these intrepid nuns to organize. "Beds, but just for the three children. I'll be glad just to collapse into any available chair."

Agnes placed a finger to her lips to warn me to keep silent. She closed the flap and disappeared. Long minutes later Agnes returned with another novice. This time both novices wore their regulation linen head gear with no hair visible.

Gesturing to follow them inside past the opened flap, which I secured promptly, both novices kept fingers to their lips.

Silently we crept past sleeping nuns. They were boxed in separated cubicles. These cells were created by nothing more than curtains hanging wall-like such as I'd seen in hospitals' mixed wards.

The older nuns snored. One young nun wasn't asleep, she was hiding under the sheets reading a book by flashlight.

My orphans behaved well. None played up, or made faces.

When finally we emerged into a second tent we entered a separate cell where the Reverend Mother was at her prie-dieu saying the rosary. It would be **there** that the children finally started to giggle.

Not angry at being disturbed, the stooped Reverend Mother tried to stand and greet us, but wobbled. I rushed forward to take her arm. She didn't push it away. A very tall woman whose flesh had sagged, she pulled herself up like a stork. She smelled of starch for her coif.

Her face crinkled into a wide smile and all the wrinkles seemed more pronounced. Her eyes danced like fireflies. "Lovely to see you, dear little Ella," she said in Oxford-honed English. "But why so late? I heard that the Director was evicting you hours ago."

I laughed. "Your telegraph system of novices carrying messages still works! Yes. Evicted! I'm afraid nighttime caught up with us. I went to see the stand-in for a new Administrator, to plead he'd leave me in my cottage."

"That nice Ray Bruce? He can't help you. He has no official position. His title of interim-Administrator? A joke! In this area, when a man isn't earning a substantial salary, he's a nobody."

I led the Reverend Mother to sit down on the only chair. She seemed in great spirits. I'd noticed on earlier occasions how much she enjoyed having visitors.

Educated conversation was as necessary to this elderly nun as is a fix to a drug addict.

Most of her sister nuns came from backward farms. Not much in the way of rewarding conversation from them! Anyway, cozying up to other nuns was strictly forbidden by this Order, probably due to unhappy past messes. Not like Carmelites, they weren't forbidden visits, but there weren't many visitors in Darfur of the Reverend Mother's intellectual caliber.

I'd felt I was lacking in just that on the occasions I'd met her before. But my Lloyd had been a great debater for her to cross words with.

CHAPTER 4

Now she astonished me by tackling a totally unexpected subject. "My dear, have you been approached to sell your eggs?"

I knew she wasn't referring to chicken eggs: there weren't any chicken eggs in Darfur, chickens would be eaten too fast here for them to lay eggs.

My eggs?

I didn't know much about a market for human eggs. I sent a watery smile in the Reverend Mother's direction. I hated to sound

ignorant.

She pressed on grimly. "Great advances have been made for new uses for women's eggs at Imperial College in London, and at the Wolfson at Cambridge. Infertility due to damaged or sick ovarian eggs may be a problem of the past." While speaking she gestured to Agnes to steer the orphans to another tent to find their beds. And maybe to send them away from such a fraught conversation?

Alone with me, Reverend Mother continued: "There's been a considerable market for healthy eggs for some years in Europe and America. Our greedy African entrepreneurs weren't left far behind. But they've added another dimension to this ugly trade: they want the eggs of white women for rich blacks who want to whiten their lineage.

Considerable money is involved when large quantities of healthy eggs are marketed."

"Why do you call it an ugly trade? Isn't it wonderful for a sterile woman to be able to have a child?"

"I'm not going to touch on the theological aspect. Right now I'm concerned for the girls approached in this very camp for that use. You understand, the girls who sell their eggs may become infertile themselves after disease or infection destroys their ovaries."

"Disease! Infection!" I wanted to make an intelligent comment, but I felt trounced. Not a hypochondriac, but I've always been over-aware of germs. Hardly a sensible trait in a refugee camp!

"I've had two sweet girls come to my tent just this week pleading for a place to live because they'd been homeless and had sold their ovary's eggs, and were consequently suffering serious infections."

Listening intently, my mind jumped to the loss of Lloyd's heart. Could there be a connection? Eggs for sale! Hearts for sale! Had Reverend Mother deliberately led me to make a connection?

"I'd like to meet those two girls," I said very quietly.

"I thought you might. One has left me to travel to Ethiopia. Bertha, the younger girl is still here." The Reverend Mother's eyes grew sad: "I imagine you see a connection between the trade in eggs and the trade in body parts."

She rang a sweet-tinkling bell. Agnes reappeared. The Reverend Mother's orders were brief. "Take Ella to meet Bertha. Inform Bertha she's to tell her all she knows."

No kiss or other physical way of saying goodbye from the Reverend Mother. We bowed to each other and with a sigh she returned to her prie-dieu, unhooked the rosary from her belt and began to pray as she fingered the beads.

I followed Agnes. She opened flaps. The first one led to a kitchen tent. The next to a playschool tent. Another to the novices' tent. One last flap and we reached the farthest tent. It had one bunk bed.

A red-headed girl with a size 46 bust was reading by candlelight in the lower bunk. "Bertha?" I asked.

She nodded. Agnes introduced me, passed along the Reverend Mother's orders, and left us.

Bertha was a most extraordinary red-head. Her red hair continued down her neck to her arms and the visible parts of her fat belly. Her legs were bent, revealing thick red hair all the way up to her thighs. Mixed in with the hair were large freckles that had melded together to form amoeba-shaped blotches. Her eyes were a faded blue like the Norwegian skies of her homeland.

She looked up from her book with resignation. "Yes?" she asked.

Bertha had no intention of offering to answer questions as Reverend Mother had wished.

I squatted on the far side of her mattress. I tried my warmest smile. "Could you talk to me about the sale of women's eggs?"

She asked: "Have any cigies? Not allowed inside the tent but we can sneak outside for a fag."

"Sorry, no. I traded for food the ones left by my husband. He was a smoker. Marlboros."

"That was Lloyd Phelps? The one who was murdered, and had his heart stolen?" Bertha was certainly blunt.

"Yes. And I'm flat broke. His salary was due the week after."

"Didn't you and your husband adopt some orphans?"

"Yes. Well, not officially. We took in three. I love them."

"All of us want to take in these orphans. Like unwanted puppies left on highways after Christmas. But none of us can afford them. How will you educate them? Send them away to your fancy British schools at twenty thousand pounds a year for each?"

"We'd planned to teach them ourselves. We both had degrees in education."

"No rich parents to pay for your craving to be the big generous philanthropists?"

"My parents have been dead for donkeys' years. Poor Lloyd had only just lost his in an auto accident in the Cumbrian Mountains. No money inherited. There was barely enough for their funeral expenses after shipping their bodies back to the family plot. House reclaimed by the mortgage company. Their car a write-off wreck."

"So you can't really afford the luxury of being a great philanthropist to your orphans! And what do you want from me? I imagine it's how to get in touch with the bastards who took my eggs." Bertha left her bunk bed to search under it for the used butt of a discarded cigarette. She kept her face averted: what was she hiding?

After some scratching, she found a butt, went outside, lit it, smoked it, and not until the last drawn-out puff did she return to where I still sat on her mattress. "Okay. No good telling you in Norwegian. Of course you don't speak Norwegian. Or do you?"

"No."

"I'll start at the beginning. You'll have to hear all of my story, or none of it. Okay? Okay!"

"Sure."

"I'd always wanted to come to Africa as a missionary. But my local church wouldn't help and so I wrote away to come as a self-paid volunteer. I collected from friends for my ticket, to Chad, actually. But when I heard the crisis here was even worse, I took a bus to Nyala and from there hitched a ride in a refrigerated truck."

"Refrigerated!"

"You're getting close. Okay. So I guessed there wasn't much in the way of frozen food or meat coming into this camp, and when I put that to the driver he laughed through his gold teeth and asked me straight out if I wanted to sell my eggs."

"But you didn't need money."

"Not then I didn't. Still got my allowance in Chad. Here, though, my funds from my family failed to arrive. After all, there's no proper road or mail service into this camp. When I got really hungry, I went in search of that driver."

"Where did the operation take place?"

"If you can call it that. He'd told me he'd return to the depot in a month. I went to the depot, and he introduced me to a horrible old woman who asked questions. 'Had I ever had a baby? What diseases had I had? Did I have regular periods?'"

"You answered all those questions!" I began to feel squeamish.

"I did. No baby, but I'd been pregnant. Had an abortion when the father didn't want to know. At least he hadn't given me a disease: I was clear enough then.It was after several egg harvests that I began to cry *down there* all the time, with pus and a thick white fluid coming out non-stop. Of course, the periods stopped after a while. That was the end of my doing business with them."

Now, listening to Bertha I felt sick. I would have vomited but there was no toilet in the tent to throw up into.

Controlling that urge, I offered her a hand to squeeze, but she roughly shoved it aside. What next? Did she think I was a lesbian, having invaded her tent at night and trying to grab at her?

No. Bertha simply wanted another smoke. She dug around the tent's corners, sending off a cockroach, and found another fag end. She left me to go outside to puff what little nicotine she could eke out of the butt.

Again, I waited to learn more.

She delivered. Smelling her tobacco-stained fingers for whatever pleasure they gave her, she continued: "You can find that old female witch-doctor near the depot. The locals call her Ma Belle. Doesn't mean My Beauty. God knows she's anything BUT! Ma, here in mid-Africa, means a married woman. Ma Belle squats under the only tree left in that area. As you may have noticed, all trees and bushes have been chopped down by the refugees to make struts for their plastic-covered lean-tos or for thatch.

"She must be very powerful, to have kept that tree for her shade."

"Powerful? I suppose so. More likely Baku wants to keep her in good health so she gets the eggs for him."

"Baku! I've heard that name."

"Big entrepreneur in these parts. Doesn't miss a trick. Not one that will make a profit for him. Money talks around here, you know."

"Doesn't it everywhere?" I said gloomily. "How can I meet this Baku?"

"You can't. You're small fry. Too small. But I heard from Agnes that you talked back to the Director. You've got guts."

"It didn't do me any good. He won't let me get a job or another cottage."

"I heard from Agnes that you also talked back to the stand-in for the Administrator who hasn't yet arrived. Ray Bruce! He's a dish, isn't he? But close mouthed. I stood in the sun for three hours with dozens of others to ask for help. He dismissed me with two words: "Can't help."

I recalled that I thought he was too brief when he dealt with me. But what a difference! In fact he had spoken of his three orphans, and detailed four refugee camps. Now I knew I'd read him wrong.

My heart leaped. All the loneliness I'd endured since Lloyd's murder swelled inside me and then seemed to drop away like pain after taking a super strong aspirin.

Could he have found me attractive? With my lank hair and emaciated features! I remembered that while on one plane my mind had been focused on housing for my orphans, on a deeper more hidden plane I'd resented his healthy look yet dreamed of being kissed.

Bertha hooted: "When I mentioned Ray Bruce, you lit up like you're being laid. Don't waste all that girlie passion on a non-entity. A man without a salary isn't a man. Now if you really want someone to dream about, there's his flat-mate Bernard Laplante."

I countered Bertha's know-all comments. "He's one of the Medecins Sans Frontieres. They're volunteers too."

"Okay. But Bernard Laplante's got money. Inherited? Earned it in private practice? Who cares? Money!"

Agnes reappeared. "Reverend Mother has put out her candle. Everybody's candle must be put out. Bertha, have you been smoking in this tent? Smells like it."

"No. I'm not so stupid. Or to give up my tent to this woman! It was enough I told her where to sell her eggs."

"Bertha, Reverend Mother wants you to share the tent with Ella. There's a bunk bed. She can take one of the bunks." Agnes adjusted her cowl and left them in the dark. Agnes would never have attempted to disobey Reverend Mother: she couldn't imagine anyone disobeying her. Agnes's footsteps wafted away through a night still broken by howls from hungry children and abused women. Agnes knew that terrible crimes were committed against women in the camp, but she was totally uninformed about sexual deviations and resisted learning about the horrors women endured in nearby lean-tos Their screams did not slow her departure.

Bertha had no qualms about the happenings outside: she had been the victim herself on too many occasions. After a particularly gruesome scream, she complained: "Why can't the men just fuck?"

I lost my foothold trying to climb up to the upper bunk. "Oh! Could you light a match, please?"

Grumpily, Bertha complied. She didn't waste a chance to complain. "My last match!"

I swung my leg over the upper bunk's restraining board. In the eerie light of the petering match, I gathered impressions. One lumpy mattress. No pillow. No sheets. No crucifix at the head. No holy picture. A vertical slit in the canvas partition leading to the novices' cells. Peeling paint. Dirt floor. A trench for rain water. The leather flap serving as a door. A nail for Bertha's Norwegian raincoat. No table. No chair. No desk. No carpet. No lamp, not even a kerosene lantern. A pottery bowl empty of water: cracked, it may have let its water escape. One candle, extinguished: no holder. A heavily thumbed book with a lurid cover. Bertha.

The match guttered and its flame died.

Bertha began to snore, not heavily, making a purring sound like an old cat.

I didn't sleep. I felt exhausted, my bones ached and a pain shot up from my heels. I rubbed them against the lumps in the mattress. No good. My heels were a familiar problem, often hurting me before. I knew there existed a salve for heels. I didn't have any.

I began to weep. I thought of Lloyd and how happy we had been lying in each other's arms. Sometimes his hands had hurt my breasts, but I had never asked him to stop caressing them. How I wished he was with me now, and that I could feel his fingers bringing me alight to arousal.

For a fleeting moment, Ray Bruce's face flashed in my mind. No! I told myself I could not be so ridiculous as to long for a man I had met only that day for such a few brief moments.

I whispered into my old coat I'd chosen to use as a sheet, 'I won't cheapen myself, giving away to thoughts of someone other than Lloyd."

My tears continued to work through the grime on my face. When had I become so weak? "Lloyd, oh Lloyd!"

I finally fell asleep to the sounds of bleating children.

CHAPTER 5

There were no roosters to wake the people in this camp. It was the shuffle of hundreds of feet tramping the dust in search of water that woke me. Desperate voices mumbled, all with the same plea: "Where cawater?"

The children's cries were more urgent. I leaped up in my upper bunk, and hit my head hard on the low ceiling.

I listened to the voices' pleas and the children's stifled braying. These did not come from my orphans, I didn't recognize any of the cries. But I smoothed my dress, pulled my comb from my carry bag and tidied my hair. No water for brushing my teeth. I made do with the dried out toothpaste. I took care to get a proper foothold to climb out of the upper bunk, and, without interrupting Bertha's purring snores, I lifted the leather flap and went in search of my orphans.

Agnes stopped me. "Aren't you coming to matins?"

"Uh, Good morning! No, I'm looking for my children." "Reverend Mother will expect you at matins." Agnes scurried off in the direct of the makeshift chapel, erected in one of the Order's larger tents. I dreaded matins, but there seemed no way out of following her lead and entering the chapel tent to kneel.

There was a soothing smell of incense, very welcome because it somewhat hid the outside's smells of decaying bodies and moldy tents.

The nuns sang sweetly, as if they were still in Belgium in a fine church. Their cowls were spotless, because they had not yet ventured into the dust outside. I stared at their feet: the Order obliged them to wear sandals and usually their toes were blackened with grime and dog mess.

This early in the morning most of the nuns had clean feet. Their hands matched, although I noticed some of the more elderly nuns had dirty fingernails.

The congregation wasn't clean. None of us had any water with which to bathe the parts most urgently in need of soap and water.

Rancid perspiration lent an added odor to the ever-present smell of unwashed womanhood. No deodorants available in Darfur camps!

There were no children in the chapel. Their services had been curtailed. Wise Reverend Mother had decided not to make the children pray on empty stomachs. I thought that if and when there should appear sufficient food to satisfy the children who had suffered a lengthy spell of have-not, then she would probably institute a half hour of hymns.

My knees began to hurt in addition to my heels. I struggled to find a comfortable position as I knelt, but my mind was as miserable as my heels and knees.

The absence of children in the chapel had indicated to me that the nuns were short of food for their little guests. I wondered how I could provide breakfast for my orphans if Reverend Mother had run out of the wherewithal to feed her own charges.

I remembered that Felko, one of my smarter orphans, had lugged along our pot which had been bubbling with our maize lunch. There couldn't be anything left of that meal. I'd seen the three children partitioning and then devouring the remains while I'd visited Lloyd's plot in the graveyard.

Never one to eat a huge breakfast, now in that bare chapel I longed for bacon, eggs, marmalade, and coffee; failing those wonders, I would have settled for half a slice of moldy bread. When a bell tinkled announcing Holy Communion was on offer, I rushed to the altar rail for the wafer. But mine had been broken in two in order that those available would be sufficient to go around to all the communicants who had suddenly appeared.

Dejected, hungry, feeling I needed a bath, I stumbled out of the emptying chapel. Agnes was lurking at the outer flap. "I buried a container of Quaker Oats. If you come with me, I'll show you where it's hidden. For your orphans."

I followed meekly. I was ashamed of the boiling anger I'd felt toward the nuns when I watched them all file up to take communion.

Agnes took a roundabout route away from the prying eyes of the camps' refugees. She had planted the container under a slight depression created for garbage bags.

The depression was empty of garbage. Hyenas, or children, had gone off with whatever crumbs had been left there the night before. Not even scraps littered the dirt. It was bare, and had no telltale marks from recent scooping up any remains.

To hide her own digging, Agnes erected a wide piece of plastic. That took some doing: for barriers Agnes made use of two abandoned water barrels. The plastic had been rescued from one of the convent's cells.

From behind this makeshift curtain I obeyed her suggestions of where to dig. Soon my fingers felt a round surface: the container's top. Almost hysterical, I plunged my hands deep into the unwieldy dry soil. Scratching, pulling, I dragged out the container. It was entire. No holes, no cracks had sullied its contents.

"Dieu merci," Agnes sighed.

"Yes, thank God for this," I agreed in a whisper. "But where do we get water to boil the oats? Matches and firewood? I've got a pot. Can we cook in the convent's kitchen?"

Agnes shook her head. "This is a small container. If we take it to the convent there won't be enough for even a spoonful for each nun and all the convent children. I wish it was more: my family sent it to me through Chad. I've been saving it for Christmas." Agnes dropped her voice for her last admission, as if she was ashamed of keeping the oats for herself, but wanting to make sure that I didn't think she had stolen the container from the convent's pantry.

"Come on. Let's go locate my orphans." I tried to find the route to return toward the convent. Agnes had completely miscalculated. and

I had to lead the way, because Agnes had hung back to hide the oats' container by wrapping it in the bulky plastic curtain.

Agnes slowed our pace. Immediately a pack of street children pulled at the plastic curtain. A plastic curtain was an essential commodity in the camp, providing privacy and some protection from the elements when used as a wall for a lean-to. As Agnes tugged hard to retrieve the plastic, her container dropped, its cover opened and some of the oats spilled into the trail's dirt. Children swarmed to scoop up oats with their fingers, appearing suddenly from all corners like starlings heading for a tree with fruit. Agnes dug into the dirt to save some of her oats.

The street children shoved mouthfuls of dirt into their mouths to savor one grain of oats.

Appalled, I tried to save the container. I recognized these children's urgent need for food, but my own orphans had a prior claim to my heart. Like a windmill in a gale, I went for the container and its remaining contents, elbowing and stomping.

"What's all this?" Ray Bruce appeared within yards of us and strode into our end of the trail. I looked up through the rising dust to meet his eyes. I clutched at the retrieved container, but somehow felt ashamed of my performance. I unwound my arms from when they had flayed the children to get at the container. Oh! My vulva started acting up again. I couldn't say a word.

Agnes spoke for both of us. Her Flemish accent sounded strange here. "Sir, we were trying to save a Christmas present sent to me by my family. Ella needs food for her children."

Coldly, Ray Bruce said: "And these children need food too. I haven't many rolls, but they are welcome to these." He opened a large hand to untie the strings of a bag he was carrying. He tossed rolls in every direction like popcorn from a vending machine, not missing any of the huddled children. Hands' pink palms caught at the rolls as if the owners were baseball pros. Not one roll hit the dirt.

As the children munched at the fresh bread, Ray escorted Agnes and me toward the convent. "Looks like you could use a bit of convoying," he remarked in a controlled voice.

Agnes busily rearranged her tilted whimple, folded the plastic curtain, and took back the container. The little novice had learned the street ways of this camp and had no intention of being attacked again.

She kept up with Ray's long strides, and piped into conversation like a nursery child sings along with a teacher.

"Yes, a convoy! And thank you, Mr. Bruce for coming to our rescue. And how are you, Mr. Bruce? Are you comfortable sharing the bungalow with Monsieur Laplante?

"Very comfortable, thank you, Sister. Particularly as I believe he doesn't intend to be here in the camp very often. Can I help you with that curtain?"

"Oh, no, no. I'll be returning it to the convent in a few minutes. Excuse me for asking, Mr. Bruce, but could we cook the oats in your bungalow? Have you enough water?"

"Some water. And Laplante has a sterno stove. Would it be all right for you, Sister, to come into the bungalow?"

"Non. Pas possible. But Ella can round up her orphans and she can come."

We had reached the outer perimeter of the convent on its far side where my orphans were housed.

Out of breath, and feeling deeply embarrassed I did not grasp the nettle of Ray's offer. My head low, hiding my eyes, I said: "I hear my orphans. They sound upset."

Agnes chirped, "Of course they're upset. They think you've abandoned them. But just wait until they see what you have broughtthem!"

Ray asked: "Sister, aren't you going to eat with us?"

"Our Order forbids that. But I see you have a handkerchief, Mr. Bruce. Maybe you'd let me use it to pour out a few oats for myself."

Ray, smiling broadly, untucked his handkerchief from his shirt pocket. With a gallant sweep, like a knight at a medieval tournament honoring his lady, he offered the handkerchief to Agnes. She took it quickly and shook out a handful of oats. "Goodbye, then. I'll wash it and return the handkerchief later. I'll leave it outside your bungalow's door."

Agnes called to my orphans and then left it up to Ray to choose the route to his bungalow. To my astonishment, Ray took a long way to return home. I thought: could it be that he wants to be with me as long as possible?

We left the clutches of lean-tos and freestanding reed houses and approached an open space on the camp's perimeter.

A crowd of onlookers had gathered to watch a pack of wild dogs fight an old hyena. When Ray and my orphans joined the spectators, more of the camp's refugees crowded in, with faces as alight as if they were latecomers hurrying to an opera house.

The hyena had its hackles upright like the spines of a hedgehog. Its fangs were broken, and some pivotal ones were missing. When the lead dog jumped him and took a bite out of his spotted hide, the hyena let out a yelp that was far different from the famous hyena laughter. More of the dogs closed in when they saw that the hyena was too weak to counter them. One dog after the other bit off pieces of the hyena's hide until it keeled over like a sinking canoe. All the dogs closed in and ripped open his stomach, going at it like hogs to a trough.

"Come on, let's go," Ray said brusquely. "If this is what our camp offers in the way of entertainment, I've seen enough. We should spare the children from watching this unadulterated cruelty."

I barely kept pace with his long strides. The three orphans lagged behind to watch the dogs' last forays, the dogs' jaws dripping with bits of flesh soaked in blood. The orphans ran giggling to catch up to Ray, as unconcerned by the cruelty they had witnessed as if they had been ancient Romans watching a gladiator die.

Reaching his bungalow, Ray said hesitantly: "Maybe I should not ask you to come in. Your visit here might be misinterpreted."

I giggled. "I've been married, Mr. Bruce. I'm not a young girl."

"I wasn't referring to your marital status. This isn't really my bungalow. I'm here on Laplante's say-so."

I pushed open the outside door and went in to look around. The bungalow contained two rooms. One, lightly furnished, was a bedroom. It had a single camp-bed, one small bedside table, a kerosene lamp and nothing else. Ray Bruce's?

Laplante obviously lived in the second room, a parlor that had been fitted with a sofa-bed. In this room were several antique mahogany tables. On one a valuable collection of African wood carvings circled around a priceless Benin cire perdu sculpture of a pregnant female. On another table a laptop computer and a battery-operated TV shared space with a collection of writing paper pads.

I stared at one of the pads. It was yellow and had horizontal stripes. A kerosene lamp had been left on nearby and I could read the writing on the pad plainly.

The writing was down two columns. The first column read BODY PARTS. The second read ORGANS.

I gasped. Ray, who had followed me inside and was lighting the can of sterno in a makeshift grate, turned at the sound. His glance followed mine and he turned over the pad.

Felko, who with great pride had lugged my pot from the convent, now felt as if he were the First Mate of a ship about to sail. He handed over the pot to Ray: "Pot very hard to save in camp," he grinned, with his air of a ship's officer ordering cast-off. "You have water for to boil?"

With the sterno's flame steadying, Ray left it to cross to a rustic table that held a large pottery jug. He used its dipper to ladle out enough water into my pot for the remaining oats, brought them to boil, and dug around to find eight bowls. He called to his own three orphans, still asleep in a new tent just beyond the bungalow. Clearing their eyes from a residue of mucous mixed with the ever-present dust, his three orphans looked longingly at the pot. They could smell the cooked oats, and the older ones could count that there were eight bowls set out.

Delight and hope lit their faces. Two children hugged Ray's knees. He portioned out the oats into the eight bowls and then enchanted everyone by producing a small tin of syrup.

I desperately wanted to re-read the columns of writing on the yellow pad, but my intuition warned me not to antagonize Ray. Also I felt unbearably hungry and couldn't bring myself to miss out on my bowl of oatmeal.

No one spoke while they sucked at their spoons for the last taste of the oats and syrup.

When the last child had swallowed his spit regurgitating it to enjoy the food twice, Ray's three orphans ran off to the outside tent and my children went with them. There in the dust Ray's three shared several tattered comic books and mine were introduced to their first comics.

Ray's children had so heavily fingered these comic books that the pages were in tatters but the five boys were proud to share.. These books were their treasure, but they were not brought up to be selfish and enjoyed passing them around to my three. My orphans couldn't read, but they followed the stories according to the cartoons' sketches.

Left alone with him in the bungalow, I sent a pleading look to Ray. He had remained standing, leaving the one highly-carved stool for me. He understood my message, but remained impassive and didn't turn over the pad to give me a chance to study it again.

He said: "Laplante and I are here to help eradicate polio. I resigned as an Administrator from my first post because there was not enough hygiene in the camp to combat that disease effectively. Laplante has widened his interests."

"So I saw."

"You saw some lists. I saw them too. He doesn't hide them because he must be working to find out about a market in body parts."

"I want to find out about that market too. I have myreasons."

"Yes. I heard you do. I've heard the story about your husband's heart having disappeared. But let me tell you a little about our projects." Ray changed the subject. "Laplante and I want to help create a new, better Africa. Laplante and I both belong to Rotary Clubs, ours were part of the great scheme that rotaries have to end polio."

"Scheme?"

"Yes. Rotary has raised two and half billion for that by bringing this need to the attention of governments. Two billion children have been immunized in one hundred and twenty-two countries. But when you get right in with the children in these Sudanese refugee camps you find filthy water or practically no water, no decent latrines, and, most importantly, no facilities for immunizations. We're stopped by Sudan's central government from delivering the vaccine to Darfur, or from bringingchildren to clinics."

I listened attentively. I wasn't merely interested in the subject matter. With my vulva still wetting, I wanted to know as much as possible about Ray Bruce.

I'd been learning how much Ray enjoyed enumerating. Yesterday he'd told me about the four camps he visited. Now it was talk of billions this and billions that.

"What do you hope personally to be able to do in this god-forsaken hole?"

"For one thing, I want to make certain that the *vaccine* arrives that we bought. And properly transported in refrigerated trucks. The Sudanese Government doesn't comply with international standards where they're concerned."

I gasped. Refrigerated trucks tolled loud. But I stuck to the main subject Ray had broached. "You're saying there's money for vaccine and refrigerated trucks, but this Sudanese government stops them from reaching the camps? How can you help if it's a political problem?"

"I'm simply a member of a rotary club who wants to help. I have no political agenda, no religious or racial hang-ups. I just want to save kids from catching polio."

I stood up. I sighed, then asked quietly: "Can I have my pot, please? Shall I wash up the bowls and spoons?"

"Sorry, our ceramic jug contains all the water we've been allocated this week. I'll wipe the bowls clean. Here's your pot." Ray used a clean cloth and wiped it dry. As he transferred my pot to me, our fingers touched. I felt electric charges course through my vagina.

I showed little control, yet I managed to gulp out a few words: "I hope to see you again, Ray. To be truthful, I want to know more about the refrigerated trucks. And I need to learn where Bernard Laplante goes when he leaves this camp."

Ray stayed silent. He collected the ten bowls, keeping busy. When he spoke, he tried a basic subject: "The only clean latrine in this section of camp is just past the next two bungalows. Your orphans may need to use it after their breakfast. Goodbye. Let me know if and when you get some more oatmeal." He lifted the latch on the bungalow's door. The gesture meant goodbye.

Outside, I had to pause. My vulva was acting up. WHAT WAS HAPPENING TO ME! I was opening up *down there*. Oh God, I haven't even looked at another man these past months, mourning Lloyd full time. Now this? Having these sex urges for a man who will take for his polio program the funds needed for our AIDS work! And I was YEARNING for this man? A man I'd only seen for minutes. What urges would I get if I'm ever with him for half an hour! My brain told me that this man was using his position to pursue his own agenda. Why is it that my flesh calls out for him? That *down there* I ache to be caressed by him. ENTERED.

Feeling giddy, I led my orphans away from their three new friends' tent. I reminded myself that a fellow student at Newcastle had told me that Dames at Eton had the responsibility of seeing that the charges from their houses had a daily bowel movement. Forcing thoughts of Ray from my mind and the lust for Ray from my body, I led my three orphans to the latrine.

CHAPTER 6

Bertha was screaming.

I'd been waiting for my three orphans beside the stinking latrine.

I'd been trying to think of anything other than the over-powering suffocation caused by holding my sullied breath.

I'd felt so desperate for the third of my orphans to emerge from the latrine's reeded enclosure.

Then I heard Bertha's shrieks.

All three orphans froze. They had been trying to clean their backsides with leaves, but they pulled up their shorts and stared at Bertha. She was dragging herself down the lane towards the latrine. Her shrill cries were terrible to hear.

Terrible for me, terrible for my children.

I darted toward Bertha. I grabbed her outstretched arm as soon as I noticed Bertha's injuries.

We reached the latrine. I saw fresh blood gushing from between Bertha's legs. "What can I do to help you?"

No reply. More screaming.

"Don't go into that disgusting latrine! In your condition you'll get an infection."

Howls from Bertha. But she remained outside.

She began to shiver. She went into shock.

I hesitated. How could I call for a doctor?

An ambulance?

I turned to Felko. "Give me our pot. Run as fast as you can to the convent. Ask for Reverend Mother. If she won't see you, try to get the novice, Agnes. Run!"

I sent my other two orphans to find Ray Bruce. I knew his cottage was only two lanes away.

"Don't ask Ray Bruce to come!" Bertha interrupted her screams to whimper. "Not him!"

"Shhh. Keep your strength. Ray Bruce is a doctor."

"No. I think, I think, I think he's a dish. I don't want him to see me this way!" Bertha's gasps came mixed with repetitious murmurs.

I tried to clean Bertha's thighs. I had nothing to use that was really sanitary. My own underslip hadn't been washed in a week. But I tore a circular strip from its base and sopped up the most noticeable blood. It smelled unhealthy. This was no natural monthly flow. Bertha was hemorrhaging.

Ray appeared promptly. From the dark interior of his room he had brought a battered medical bag. He knelt in the dust next to Bertha, who was writhing in agony. I'd managed to lower her into the feotal position.

Snapping open his medical bag, Ray removed neat swabs. He opened Bertha's legs and applied them. My two orphans stared.

Bertha moaned. She kept her eyes clamped shut. Obviously she wanted to blank out what was happening.

Strangely, Bertha had come out into the heat of this morning carrying her Norwegian jacket. Why? Now she cradled it in her arms like a security blanket. Her screams had been reduced to yelps mingled with moans. Ray wrapped her in a warm plastic cover he had brought from the cottage.

She was weeping: streams of tears washed through the caked dust on her face.

As she came out of shock, Bertha tried to cover her face with her jacket. Ray gently pulled it to one side.

"When did you eat last?" he asked.

Choking noises. Bertha's tears redoubled.

An emaciated local woman, draped in a green print cotton sari-like garment, a pagan Bonti, croaked: "Woman try steal cigarettes. Meat. Manioc. Arachides. Witch doctor kick her in stomach. She bleed."

Ray sighed. "I'd have gladly given her my bowl of oatmeal." He raised Bertha's head and prepared her to receive some medicine he had taken out of his bag. Ray eyedropped some liquid between her clenched teeth.

Bertha became calmer. I wondered if Ray had administered laudanum, or was that still permitted with its opium base?"

Agnes arrived with another novice. "An ambulance will come soon. Reverend Mother sent several of us to various hospitals to plead for one." The little novices held on to their fluttering wimples which were like white butterflies in a high wind.

I breathed more easily. Once again I felt grateful for the convent's bush telegraph system worked by the novices.

The novices seemed to accomplish more through their web than any other means of communication. Here, cellular phones were of no use because there was no electricity with which to charge them. Word of mouth from one novice to another was the means I would always favor.

But when the ambulance arrived, I lost my composure. It was the same makeshift vehicle that had transported Lloyd.

It was filthy. Its paint peeled to show old layers of rust. One window was shattered, another had its split pane stuck together with masking tape. The tires didn't match, causing a lopsided careening, lurching motion.

Ray climbed into the ambulance once Bertha had been settled on a gurney. I joined them, crouching like a red indian next to a fire. I took Bertha's right hand. Bertha tore it from my grasp.

Bertha's energy was returning, although masked by the laudanum. She was gritting her teeth, not speaking. Her eyes were clamped shut. But her bleeding had eased, stanched by Ray's swabs.

Before the vehicle revved its motor to leave the scene, I called out to my three orphans who had returned: "Go back to the convent with Agnes."

I concentrated my attention on Bertha, once the vehicle began its halting journey. Bertha rejected me, slapping away my open hand.

Ray gave his professional opinion: "You'll be all right. If we getyou to the right clinic, you can have some antibiotics. I'll prescribe them. Haven't got any in this kit I brought. Mostly it's vaccines."

In a ghostly voice, Bertha shocked him. "I have Aids. You got my blood on you."

Ray didn't blink.

I blinked.

I had come to Africa to work with AIDS patients. And yet I hadn't guessed what Bertha's worst nightmare was. I had spent the night in her bunk bed, listened to her complaints and story, but never entered AIDS into the quotient. I had no fear of AIDS for myself. Lloyd and I had discounted the percentages of either of us becoming infected through our work. But suddenly I found myself cringing at the way Bertha had revealed her disease to Ray. Was shegloating that perhaps she had infected him? Certainly I'd heard of several instances where a quantity of blood from an AIDS patient had infected an attending doctor. Bertha had pleaded not to let Ray attend to her. "Not that dish Ray!"

I couldn't tear off another piece from my underslip to clean Ray's hands. My dress was too transparent and I'd be as naked as a debutante at a garden party wearing only a nylon dress when caught in a cloudburst.

He didn't need my help. Again he snapped open his medical bag and this time removed anti-septic lotion and more of the swabs. Silently, with no dark look on his open face, he removed the stains from Bertha's blood. He offered me the same bottle and swabs.

I thought to shake my head in refusal, but then recalled that one way to lose a new friend was by turning down a kindness offered. I swabbed at my fingers.

I said: "Bertha, thank God you've told us. Ray can help, and I can help too. My former clinic has medicines that will deal with AIDS. When you're fit enough, we'll go there."

Bertha made a sorry grimace. "I've read about those medicines sent to Africa. Too old to be of any use. Past their sell-by dates."

"No." Ray said quietly. "It's true there are clinics that dispense old medicines. But I'm here to see that doesn't happen in this camp. My head office was warned, and our polio vaccine is as fresh as it's possible to get anywhere. There will be a delivery by a refrigerated truck in the next few days, and I will go personally to check out what arrives for treating AIDS."

"There'll be nothing for me. I have no pull with the Sudanese Government."

"These medicines were sent by the United Nations. Their forces have been escorting them across warlord country. You'll get enough."

"Don't you believe it. I heard that all the food and the medicine parcels sent by the United Nations were cut in half. I'll be in that other half who doesn't get any." Bertha's voice went weak again. The blood gushed. Without a qualm, Ray stanched the flow with more swabs.

I looked away.

The ambulance jerked to a halt. We weren't within any feasible distance of a hospital. The driver shouted to Ray: "You. Get out." He picked his teeth with the point of a knife that could double as a weapon, and added to me: "You too, woman."

We said quick goodbyes to Bertha and scrambled out of the so-called ambulance.

Ray read out the peeling sign on the ambulance's side: Nyala Surgery.

He said: "Nyala. That's a long way from here. Whoever bought that ambulance didn't bother to change the sign."

Neither of us bothered to complain about being left on the dusty road to cough out the carbon monoxide expelled from the vehicle.

I said: "I'm worried about Bertha. How am I ever going to find where she is?"

"One of my three orphans will track her down. The boys are good at that. They like to think they're like Superman and can manage amazing things."

I wondered. Could his three orphans compete with the Reverend Mother's bush telegraph run by her novices? I continued: "I think there's one hospital fairly near here. I can walk to it. But what about you?"

"My clinic's not far."

We entered a very different area of the camp. Here all was neat Quonset huts, ranged like miniature airport hangars in tidy lanes as beautifully laid out as Lenfant had envisioned for Washington, D.C.

The inhabitants did not look any more prosperous than where Reverend Mother had pitched the tents of her convent. Women managed to cover themselves with the bright colored cottons favored in the Sudan, but the men and children wore dull rags.

There was no sign of water or of cooking fires. Children stared at us with that haunted look due to malnutrition.

When we came to a one-room hut, Ray said: "This is it. My clinic." The hut had a window, but no glass in it, and a door with no lock.

Instead of a lock, a Moslem attendant came out of it who had been guarding the solitary table that was filled with trays of hypodermic needles, containers with swabs, and bottles of disinfectants.

There were no patients. One lone woman stood hovering nearby. Smiling at her, Ray gestured for her to come into the hut. He said to me: "She asks for injections every day. She doesn't specify what she wants them for. I think she believes anything I give her will chase away evil spirits."

"And you give her an injection every day against polio?"

"No. I did give her one, when she first started coming. Adults get polio too. Remember the American President Roosevelt, who caught it in his forties.But now I just give her a dose of glucose, and that feeds what she needs fed."

I said: "I wouldn't mind some of that."

"Actually, today must be her last dose. I've heard there are some cases of polio in the next camp. It won't take long for it to spread here. I'll need to ration everything."

"Why should it come here?"

"The refugees move around when they can. They always hope there's food or water in the next camp. Sort of like thinking there will be a harvest in the next fields. They bring polio, and tuberculosis, cholera. AIDS."

When Ray mentioned AIDS, we both became silent. Thinking. What would become of Bertha? Where would she get the money to pay for medication?

I gave a small bow to the Moslem assistant. But he ignored me, because it was time for prayers. He looked toward the sun and knelt for noon prayers without another word. But the solitary patient grinned widely to show off her gold front tooth, pressed my hands and gave a small curtsy.

Ray nodded. He looked depressed. Or maybe, just maybe, he was feeling sorry to know it was time for me to leave.

I walked and walked, my vulva shrinking like a balloon the farther I went from Ray. My heels began to clamor for rest, or ointment, or at least water to bathe my feet. I didn't stop. I looked in every lane for some indication of a hospital. None.

But I finally did come out into a wide plaza that had a leafy shade tree in its center. And under the tree, exactly as Bertha had told me, was a witch-like old woman. Ma Belle! Her two incisors stuck out of her thick lips like tusks. Her one eye squinted with malice. Every few seconds she spat out some type of betel juice.

Not two yards away from her was a parked refrigerated truck.

"Oh!" My exclamation caught the harpy's attention. "You come sell eggs?" she asked in a cracked voice.

"No. I mean, yes. I could, perhaps. What would you pay me?"

"Two hundred American dollars, if all correct. You married lady? Wear married lady ring."

"I've been married. My husband's dead."

The woman nodded as if I had given her an unexpected present on Christmas morning. "Children? You have?" Her tone indicated she took it for granted that I was a mother.

"No. No children."

"Why, no children?"

"We weren't married very long. Only a little over a year. We wanted children."

"No children. You sick. Maybe have AIDS. No good to me. Go away."

Flabbergasted, I turned to go. But that refrigerated truck held me like a magnet attracts metal. I asked: "I care for three orphans. They need meat for their supper. Could I buy meat from that truck?"

"Go, woman. No meat for you. Truck's driver, Sadam, bring stick. Hit you."

She gestured to a heavyset Moslem who approached speedily. He carried a lance-like pole with a knife fastened with leather cords at its tip. I didn't delay. But I made sure to take a route that passed beside the truck and I got a good look. It was modern, state-of-the-art and in excellent repair. Its paint was pristine, its tires new, a blast of continuous hot air came out from a duct that indicated there was air-conditioning for the driver. I scuttled alongside, gathering all the information I could suck in. When I'd passed it, I didn't look back, I hoped I hadn't drawn suspicion by my interest.

Within a few more lanes I came to a hospital. It was barely more than a field clinic, with a very long queue of patients waiting in the noon sun hoping to be admitted.

CHAPTER 7

I didn't find Bertha. But I did get a job and some manioc for my orphans' supper. I'd worked at the hospital in the blazing afternoon sun, washing bandages that could be reused. Dirty things, these used bandages, and maybe carrying disease.

When I thought I'd drop, an intern gave me another hateful duty: "Go tell that woman over there that her sister has died."

The woman was an adolescent, whose breasts were barely budding. She had brought a pot of manioc for her sister. Instead of killing the messenger, she gave me the wonderful gift of that marioc because she'd noticed I had an empty cooking pot. I remembered what Felko had said, how valuable a pot was in this camp. I whispered the old saying: 'A matter of life and death,' and thought how that certainly applied to cooking pots here. No pot, no dinner: malnutrition comes, then death.

Manioc needs to be pounded, then boiled. The little adolescent had pounded this manioc, now it was up to me to cook it. I placed my arms around the girl for a few moments to let her cry while I comforted her: I only let her go when another patient suggested I ride postillion on her son's donkey to go home. A mountain farmer, her son had fitted up a small rug as a saddle and I fitted there perfectly.

At one point during my ride, the farmer dismounted and knelt for his evening prayer. I listened to the sing song of a muezzin from the nearest mosque. And I made a prayer of my own: that the old woman under the tree had been wrong and that I was not diseased.

I had never been tested for HIV, in spite of overseeing all those long queues of would-be patients at the AIDS clinic where Lloyd and I had been employed. But I knew that my periods were regular, and I had no vaginal discharge. Were there any symptoms I'd missed?

His prayers completed, the farmer and I rode on through clumps of workers leaving their jobs, and also past those unfortunates who had no work and no food to take home.

This was the time when men filled the lanes. In the morning, there were women and children, out looking for the non-existent firewood. The Sudanese women's custom of displaying the varied colors of a palette brought a garden look to these arid lanes. But the men brought no such escape from these stark, dreary miserable lanes. The Muslims wore earth-colored ankle length skirts covered with tunics, topping their heads with non-descript turbans: there were no Arabs here with their tablecloth headgear in red or blue or green and white checks. Any Arab would have been shunned and driven out, because it was the Arab forces of the Janjaweed government-backed murderous militia that had driven these refugees to come here. The Baku and Niger men wore loincloths. Most of the Christians had on T-shirts and shorts, with some sporting tired baseball capsNot only did their choice of clothing separate them into recognizable fellowship, but I could differentiate them by their languages: mostly Arabic and baqqarah.

However, among their nineteen ethnic groups there must have been almost one hundred different dialects.

I couldn't focus on this scene: all I could think of was that my ovaries could be diseased.When my friendly farmer's donkey drew near to the Reverend Mother's circle of tents, I thanked him and dismounted. I truly needed to be with my orphans to warm my heart and chase away my demons in their loving company.

How they appreciated the sight of me with the pot full of manioc. They set to finding enough camel dung to start a fire, and with three sticks to hold the pot in the style of Hamlet's three witches,I heated the manioc. They wolfed it down and scraped the pot.

Agnes arrived at my orphans' tent just too late for us to offer her some food in thanks for the sharing of her oats. Agnes was weeping. Her wimple was askew. She had no handkerchief: she used the sleeve of her habit to wipe the mucous. She managed to gasp: "Please come to see Reverend Mother."

Vespers were long over and I sidestepped the chapel to go straight into Reverend Mother's cell. She was not praying her rosary, she was weeping. She had a handkerchief, and made noisy use of it, honking loudly as tears gushed to turn it into a wet towel. "Mea culpa," she gasped to me. "All my fault what has happened to that girl, Bertha.Mea culpa. Mine alone."

"She isn't in a hospital? Surely, in a hospital the doctors are responsible."

"Bertha's dead. She never made it to a hospital."

"She told me she had AIDS. But, dead? So soon?"

"Not from AIDS. That's not a death sentence if treatment is given. There are effective antiretroviral medicines. I could have got them for her. No. She was taken by bodysnatchers. I don't know what method was used to kill her: some way that would leave her organs and bones and the retinas of her eyes intact. Her red hair for wigs. The rest of poor Bertha was thrown to hyenas. One of my novices came on that scene of horror. She had paused to join a group of women spectators, hoping there was food for sale. She saw the hyenas devouring Bertha's remains."

I slumped to crouch on the prie dieu. "No!"

Reverend Mother's wimple was more askew than Agnes's: a coil of damp gray hair escaped from it.

She released the soaked handkerchief to adjust her headgear. "One of my other novices saw the refrigerated truck leaving the camp, late. My novice missed vespers to watch. I think Bertha's body parts were in that truck."

"But the old crone Bertha sold her eggs to, she must have known that Bertha had AIDS. Was diseased. She wouldn't buy if the person had AIDS.

Reverend Mother found a clean handkerchief among her spare wimples. Trying not to wet it too much, she controlled her weeping. "A diseased corpse will sell. The bodysnatchers will swear the bones, or ligaments, or even skin have been sterilized and that therefore the chance of passing on a disease is very negligible. Probably lies. But when a rich customer has waited a long time for a legal operation, desperate for a hip joint, a bone transplant, a retina, or whatever: that patient will go down an illegal path and take what's on offer. And without proper sterilization, yes, HIV could be transmitted."

Dully, I said: "I read that the bones of my favorite broadcaster, Alistair Cooke, were sold by a funeral parlor in America. He died at ninety-five. From cancer. What chance for a girl like Bertha?"

That remark caused another siege of weeping.Reverend Mother's second handkerchief was soaked. I felt I must disappear from this tent to collect my thoughts and mourn Bertha privately. I said a few words of condolence, and slipped out.

CHAPTER 8

I spent a sleepless night. Bertha's tent was not empty. Another Scandinavian girl had taken the lower bunk. She was weeping when I entered and continued to cry until dawn. I cried too.

Sometimes when I hear someone weeping it sets me off, just like when someone else vomits I feel queasy.

Dawn in the Sudan can be beautiful. Scarlet streaks, like islands in a calm sea, can appear from behind the brown parched mountains, brown due to the worst drought in fifty years.

This dawn was beautiful because, shortly after it began, I heard Ray Bruce's voice beyond the flap of Bertha's tent.

"Ella, I've been told the sad news. Have to be at the clinic by seven, but I wanted to offer some words of comfort. I feel guilty. So I suppose you've had twinges too. That's why I'm here. To help."

His voice woke up the Scandinavian. She stopped weeping and peered through the open flap. She liked what she saw and immediately found a comb and tidied her hair, put on lipstick, and sawed at her teeth with a tired toothpick.

I said: "Dr. Bruce, give me a minute." I wasn't going to be less tidy than this poaching Scandinavian girl, who had already popped out of her lower bunk and gone outside to introduce herself to Ray.

Tidying my hair and choosing a clean dress from all those wonders I had never used since my college days, I lost the advantage of being first to speak to Ray. The Scandinavian girl was jabbering to him, telling him her version of Bertha's story: "Silly woman, Bertha. Her parents would have paid for her to have treatment, and she could have slipped over the border to Chad with little trouble. She was asking for this."

Ray watched me emerge from the tent and his eyes lit. He gave a polite but dismissive bow to the Scandinavian girl and placed an arm around my shoulders. "I'd suggest we go somewhere for breakfast, but there isn't any such place. Coffee? I've still got some in my cottage. Not enough for our orphans, though."

"Yes, please. Coffee would be wonderful. I saved some manioc for the boys from last night's supper before they cleaned the pot, in case I don't get any more from my job today."

I nodded politely to my Scandinavian bunk-mate. Then I gave my arm to Ray. He squeezed it.

Sublime longings opened my vagina, wetting my inner thighs.

When we entered his cottage he turned to me and kissed me. I kissed him in return, opening my mouth and inviting his tongue. Our tongues played together like mating dragonflies. But I resisted his groping hands. I knew that kissing does not give AIDS. But I felt I couldn't chance giving him a life sentence in case I was infected. I went to the water jug and drew enough for two cups of coffee.

Ray didn't object to my ending his advances. Had I done the right thing? Did that light in his eyes mean he respects me more for stopping?

We drank our coffee, savoring it as if it was sex. When the cups were emptied, he wiped them clean and I walked arm-in-arm with him to his clinic. The waiting woman had to be disappointed, and I liked the gentle way that Ray dismissed her. Would he dismiss me like that someday?

I didn't go directly to my job at that hospital. Instead, I traced my old path to the AIDS clinic where Lloyd and I had served so many hundreds of would-be patients. I took my place in a queue of silent, terrified Sudanese, and waited.

The volunteer who took my blood was new. I didn't know his name. He stared with surprise that a white woman would have queued. "It may take a few days for results. We don't have the most modern of methods here."

I nodded. Didn't I know? But I said nothing, wrote my name on a label and left.

Hard days followed. I washed bandages, and carried to the incinerator those too filthy or contaminated to be reused. And felt grateful when a patient's family rewarded me with food I could take back to the nuns' compound.

My orphans were learning their ABCs and basic arithmetic in French from a novice with a Flemish accent. After these classes they joined Rays' boys for their hours of play.

Several days passed in a gray purgatory of suspense until the happy morning when the AIDS clinic gave me a paper that said NEGATIVE.

I celebrated by choosing a route that took me past Ray's cottage.

I heard male voices from beyond the door. One was Ray's. The other, Bernard Laplante's? I didn't particularly want to meet Laplante, but I had no choice when Ray recognized my step and opened the cottage door. I entered and Laplante stayed put, on the carved stool. He didn't stand up to be introduced, he held on to a glass of wine and waved that in my direction. "Bienvenue," he said, without any intonation. I thought: "No manners!"

Ray greeted me by placing both of his hands on my shoulders and then adding a long kiss. I kissed back, but not with an open mouth.

The taste of wine was on Ray's lips. It tasted wonderful. It had been many months since I'd had wine.

I was awkward in Laplante's presence. When he gestured that I could serve myself a glass of wine, I did.But I continued to feel uncomfortable. I looked for the yellow pad with its columns listing body parts and organs. It wasn't on the table. Laplante had either filed it or burned it.

While I sipped my lovely wine, Laplante unwound himself from the stool. I thought: "He moves like a snake uncoiling from a rock."

The wine finished, I noticed that Laplanate had left the cottage.

Without a goodbye.

Ray closed the opened door, and kissed me again. This time I opened my mouth and let our tongues dance again. His hand swept to my special places, and before long we were in his part of the cottage, on his camp bed, with me on top of him, making love.

CHAPTER 9

Wonder of wonders, we mated well. Our sex organs fit, our electric impulses matched. We didn't speak much, too engrossed in the wonder of it.

I could barely force myself to leave his cot. But Ray helped, he understood a lot of the emotions that were soaring inside of me. Perhaps he had many of his own. We both knew that I'd have to hurry back to my orphans.

We parted at the door, I slipped outside, ecstatic.

Returning to the nuns' compound with a lilting walk, I was not prepared for a tragedy. But one glance at my three orphans' tear-streaked faces told me I should be prepared for one.

"Felko, what is it? You're a big boy. Why are you crying?"

"Weepy, I am. Because all people weepy here. Reason say is rape. I not know word: rape, Madame Ella, I not understand. What is rape? All nuns weep because Agnes raped. What is rape?"

I swallowed, hard, to forestall my own enormous need to weep. Agnes had been a good friend to me, I felt miserable for what had happened to her, something horrible so unlike my own beautiful experience.

But, Felko was one of *my* orphans, in my care, I knew I had to answer his query with the care he deserved.

"Dear Felko," I began, tremulously, "Rape is a form of violent assault, a forcible illegal and wicked use of a body by a criminal."

"Sister Agnes not dead."

"No. But her body has been violated."

"Could my body be violated?" He shivered.

"Yes, but I'm here to be sure that doesn't happen."

"Oldest boy belonging Dr. Bruce, that boy told me in singing class I should watch Mohammed's billygoat when he put seed into Fatima's goat. He *say that* what happen to Sister Agnes. Will she give milk later?"

"Sister Agnes must have been taken *to* a hospital. I imagine that everything is being done to assure that there will be no aftereffects to what in this case is a crime."

I couldn't say any more. My own emotions were in such a muddle. Fifteen minutes ago I had been in Ray's arms, while we each had a blissful orgasm. Here, all was ugly.

With Felko still firing questions, I drew near to Reverend Mother's cell. A dignified elderly nun, whom I'd not met before, stopped me from raising the flap. "We have orders not to disturb Reverend Mother. I have only arrived a few hours ago, but I may take her place permanently."

I stepped back, extremely disturbed by her news, and would have left except that in the corner of an eye I noticed a group of nuns bearing someone on what looked like a plank. Agnes! She wasn't in a hospital. She lay on a table being carried by eight struggling nuns.

Into the forecourt drove the unpainted, iniquitous ambulance with its half-erased NYALA sign. The nuns waited until the ambulance was parked, and its back door opened, then began to try to raise the table with Agnes on it and position it inside.

"No!" I yelped, as if a viper had bitten me. Stop!"

The eight nuns looked stupefied. How dare a homeless woman tell them what to do!

A second ambulance followed into the forecourt. This was my hospital's vehicle, not pristine new but kept clean and presentable. It slowed to a stop, then made a noise that sounded like an old woman's sigh as she settled into a chair.

Ray was up front with the driver. He jumped down from his perch and added his shouts to mine. The driver of the first ambulance recognized him, and took a second look at me, then tore off in his belching vehicle.

Very gently Ray helped raise Agnes into the second ambulance. He strode toward the front passenger seat. In another minute he would have gone.

I rushed to see the convent's new head.

"Please. Let me go with Agnes! This ambulance is from the hospital where I work. I could be helpful!"

With poor grace, this dignified but unpleasant nun gave a gesture which could be interpreted as noblesse oblige, and I was permitted to climb up inside the ambulance before it pulled away.

Agnes lay with dry eyes wide open. No tears, no sniffling. But her eyes didn't move or try to find mine.

Dusk sat on the camp like a tired eiderdown. No lights, only the beams of the ambulance. Dogs barked as we passed, but there were no women or children in the lanes: they were trying to have some vestige of a meal. Into the silence I suddenly heard Agnes speak. Not to me, but to the world in general. "It was my fault I brought this shame on my Orderby grabbing every possible chance to go out into the lanes. I could not bear to miss out on a bit of action or gossip."

I took her hand. It was cold. The fingers slowly closed, like the wings of a sick bird come to rest.

"Dear Agnes, your fault? Certainly not."

"I stopped the men in a lane where they were sharing a hookah. I asked them what it tasted like. One of them said: 'I'll show you what's tasty.'"

"Oh! Was he the one who –"

Now she turned her eyes and met mine. "Can you keep a secret?"

"I'll try.But not if it means I can't give evidence to convict this man."

"It was not one man. All three did this to me. Each smelled in a different way. I could recognize the smells, but I never saw them. I kept my eyes closed. I couldn't watch! Why do you speak of giving evidence? Can I be forced to speak at a trial?"

I found these questions more difficult than Felko's. In the past few days I'd collected some information about her religious Order. Novices could be called sister, the other nuns were Mother, and at their head: a Reverend Mother. They were not cloistered, but interaction with the outside world was frowned upon. I remembered that Agnes had told me she could not eat outside the convent. What else? I had much to learn about these nuns.

I said: "Just get over the next hurdle before you worry about a trial. You'll have some unpleasant tests in my hospital, and that's more than enough horrors for today."

When we arrived at the emergency entrance, Ray helped the waiting interns to place Agnes on a modern gurney .He told them: "I want a report on this patient every day. She needs a complete disinfection program. Inside and outside. Tests for possible transmission of diseases. I'm Dr. Bruce. Your Administrator will okay my credentials." Finally, Ray turned to me. He was almost as impersonal as a team leader disbanding a group of soccer players: "I had a revealing chat with my friendly driver. I'd flagged him after my boys told me about Agnes.He was driving empty after delivering a woman-convalescent to her home. Good man. I asked him if there was news of the refrigerated van that's bringing my polio vaccine."

"And?"

"The van's here. Been waiting for dusk to sneak to another area of the camp. The driver of that refrigerated van has no intention of delivering vaccine tonight. My new friend told me that a whole thatched hut was dismantled, so its reeds and thatch could be used to camouflage the vehicle."

"That's interesting. Why camouflage something unless you want to hide it?"

"My thoughts exactly. But you'd better go along with Agnes. The local doctors might think she was an expectant mum, and add insult to her injuries." No light laugh. Not a joking matter. Ray's eyes kept that group leader look.

I didn't attempt a kiss. I heard Agnes moan, and chased after the gurney.

CHAPTER 10

I often find it surprising to see who comes to visit the sick and who doesn't. At Agnes's bedside were no nuns, no best friends from among the novices. Not allowed, I suppose.

On her first morning in the ward, who should appear to bring flowers to Agnes? Malaku. Somehow he had managed to cut two weeds that had not been eaten for food.

Agnes was pleased, but there was more than embarrassment in her reaction to Malaku. I smelt fear. I believe that after being raped she couldn't help shrinking from any man.

I'd kept tabs on what was happening in the Agnes case. There was no trail leading to the men who had committed the gang rape.

Agnes told me that she vaguely recalled there were other people in the lane. None of those people had tried to save her. No good Samaritans present.

I think that Agnes may nothave wanted to give any leads because she was determined not to appear in a court room on these charges. In a Muslim-dominated country, women who are not veiled or go in the streets unaccompanied are looked on as sexually available. Poor Agnes, in her nuns' habit she couldn't be criticized for not dressing modestly. Veils are rarely worn by Sudan's Moslem women. I'd often thought how alike the nuns' habits were to the acceptable outfits for Moslem women here. That had been of no help to Agnes, though.

Malaku brought another gift: a pot of manioc. When Agnes pleadedto excuse her for not eating from it, I was only toohappy to accept it for my orphans.

Malaku walked with me to the convent's compound to make sure I wouldn't spill any of the manioc. With his convoluted sentences, Malaku broached the subject I most wanted to hear.

"Most excellent friend, Dr. Bruce: he the icebox lorry has found this night."

"Yes. But he's very upset that his polio vaccine wasn't delivered to him immediately on the truck's arrival."

"We the lorry should visit. Maybe get ride. Maybe I find what to my brother had happened."

"I can't leave my orphans. And, Tekla?"

"I tell Tekla, 'go where I go.' Your orphans too must same route take."

We collected the children and, after they had eaten all the manioc, we led them through the dark lanes to where the refrigerated truck stood camouflaged under its wig of reeds and thatch.

Before we reached that clearing, noticeably empty of huts, I could smell hot coffee. Impossible!Here? From a truck in this camp? Then I saw the driver of the van was using his van's electric point on the dashboard to heat a cup of coffee. For entertainment, he had his van's radio softly playing Arabic music. He neither saw, nor heard us.

Malaku gestured for me to come away. I was very eager to get far from the truck before one of the children sneezed, or made a complaint. He led us down more trails.

Within sight of the Director's office there was another truck, smaller, older and without a lovely aroma of heated coffee emanating from it.

Malaku spoke to the driver in Amharic.An Ethiopian, he jumped down from his seat and hugged Malaku.

Soon the driver came to the shadows where I stood with the children. In French he invited us to climb into his truck.

Long before a new dawn we were driving up, up into the stark brown mountains looming past our camp. The truck was obviously meant to transport coffee beans because it retained their sickly sweet smell. There were vestiges of hemp bags on the floor and I portioned out the scraps to the seven children to serve as a thin mattress for each.. I should have saved a piece for myself, because each bump on the trail – and there were many – hit my spine like a hammer.

While the children dozed, I tried to assemble my thoughts. But my emotions played havoc with any sensible conclusion. I couldn't stop comparing my blissful orgasm to the agony Agnes had endured. My wonder and her horror.

In Ray's bed I'd dreamed of a new life, perhaps marriage to Ray.

On the loathsome unlit trail where Agnes had been gang raped, she must have believed her life to be ending. Would any other Order of nuns accept her if there was to be a long drawn-out trial? Or was there any chance her own Order might keep her on?

I must have dozed in spite of my anguished thoughts, because when I woke I saw very different scenery. We had come to a verdant land, with people carting foodstuffs and firewood.

Its people were friendly, and waved at us as we drove past. There were animals and birds. Which had not been eaten!

We'd traveled many hours. Most of the daylight was soon over. Already streaks of violet and mauve announced the coming of twilight. What woke me was that we had stopped to refuel and the spare gas was in the body of the truck. The doors were opened and two Ethiopian faces peered in at us, Malaku's and the driver's. I nodded, half asleep, while the two men hauled out a can of gasoline.

A nice surprise was that the driver returned with a large bag he had carried in his cab. "Arachides," he said grinning: "for the children. Not for the elephants."

Arachides, the local peanuts, would have been a treat for them at any time but now after ten hours without food the orphans cracked away at their shells with frenzy. I ate some too, and sighed because they tasted so delicious. When had my tastes so changed?

Here, in Darfur!

We were packed back into our places in the van, and it began a sharp descent. I could observe the scene below from the one window that looked on to the cab's windshield. While Malaku and the driver kept up their lengthy conversation in Amharic, I stared at what I believed to be Chad.

Our road had widened and other vehicles passed. None of their passengers appeared threatening. I worried what might happen when we reached what looked like a border crossing. But when we arrived at it our driver bypassed the border without so much as a grunt. I saw a soldier with a rifle, his fatigues very soiled. He wasn't bothering to wear his metal helmet. His army boots were filthy and broken. He couldn't have been over eighteen. I wondered at what age he could have joined the army for his uniform to be so dilapidated. Fourteen? Fifteen?

Two local women tended a herd of skinny goats. Considering all the greenery I'd seen, I couldn't understand why these goats were so skeletal. The women carried long sticks to keep their goats from straying.

There were no children. Could they still be in school at this hour, or was it customary here to feed them their dinner early?

Not far from this sloppily secured border our driver pulled up under a large poinciana tree.

This was a land where the people could afford to give space to a tree that had flowers instead of fruit. I dismounted, and helped the seven children to get their legs re-accustomed to solid ground. Personally, as if we had been aboard a swaying ship for these ten hours.

There was a banana grove within yards of us, and I suppose I should feel ashamed for permitting it, but I let the children strip bananas that must have belonged to a local farmer. I was fascinated by the way they grew, I don't think I'd ever seen before the large purple conical heads that sprouted purple leaves to cover the baby bananas.

The farmer who owned the grove came from his house and demanded payment. Our Ethiopian driver haggled with the man and finally paid him what he asked. We didn't want notoriety here.

We drove to a nearby inn. Malaku led us quietly to an enclosed terrace that hid us from curious locals. He said: "Here, prudent we must be. This town, border town. Our driver has the payment made for us to eat dinner and sleep at hostel."

"I think my boys need toilets more than anything right now. Are there any here?"

"Toilets, yes. I show. Please to be explicit the children to behave must."

"They'll only want to play. After being cooped up all those hours. I doubt they'll make any trouble."

"Trouble, no must happen. Our driver, he the answer to our questions has. He say 'After toilets, he take go next village.' There, a refrigeration plant very fine. We must see."

Malaku went herding the children while I found a modern bathroom where I could do a repair job on myself. I located running water to wash my face and half my body. I even bathed my poor feet. The prospect of a meal and a bed warranted putting on a good appearance.

When I tried to leave the bathroom, I couldn't budge the door. Locked from the outside, the door turned out to be extremely sturdy. I tried calling out in a polite voice, which -- after a while -- I tuned up to become a screech. Nobody came. I banged and kicked at the door. There was no window, the walls were cement. No escape through them.

The floor was tiled, and cool. I lay down on it, not believing that I'd come so close to having a meal only to lose it by being trapped in this toilet facility.

I could tell when night came because an electric light was turned on outside the bathroom door giving it a pale frame. No light for me.

Where was Malaku? What had happened to the children? Had they eaten? Could they have forgotten about me in the ecstasy of having a meal? No. Of course not. There had to be a plausible explanation

But, what?

I slept.

When the electric light was turned off and the pink rays of dawn now shyly framed the door, I heard footsteps. An elderly person's shuffling walk. The door was quietly unlocked, and to my dread and amazement I was staring at Ma Belle, the tusk-toothed hag who had refused my ovaries' eggs.

"You, you follow," she ordered.

Startled into obedience, I uncurled my legs and sat, then scrambled to my feet. She led me down a different corridor from the one that had invited me into captivity. It was freshly painted, smelled of disinfectant, and had glass-topped doors that opened up to a modern garage occupied by two refrigerated trucks. I recognized one of them as having been under the shade tree at our camp. It had no driver. The air-conditioning had been turned off. This time it had no smell of coffee.

Standing nearby, with the stance of a general ready to review his troops, was a well-dressed African of no distinguishable nationality or religious group. His clothes were fashionable European, probably of Italian make. His wooly hair had been let to grow to the nape of his neck in the style of a British tenor. His fingernails were clean. His hands looked as groomed as a male model's.

"I am Baku," he said, as if that was a world-famous name. He held himself very erect. "And you are Lloyd's wife."

For some reason I couldn't identify, I blushed. Maybe because in my mind I was already Ray's wife?

"I'm Ella," I said in a tone that meant I agreed. "Why was I locked overnight in a bathroom? And where are my children?"

Tusk Tooth answered for Baku. "You no children have." She spat the words. "You no good for children. Sick. Bad eggs."

"Ma Belle, please go into dinner," he spoke as if he was inviting Tusk Tooth to a banquet in a palace. Maybe he was. He turned to me: "And I imagine you must be very hungry. Please follow me."

I did. What else was I going to do? Run? Where to?

Baku strode out of the garage and toward a large bungalow. It looked like the setting for the film OUT OF AFRICA's scene where Isak Dinesen makes love to her houseguest. Maybe Baku had it copied? Was I to be the houseguest?

"Please be comfortable," he said to me, entering a formal dining room where a refectory table was laid for ten with embroidered linen, Tiffany silverware, Baccarat crystal goblets and limoges china. All the table settings were embossed with a huge B, which I supposed was for BAKU.

Tusk Tooth had disappeared, hopefully to choke on a dinner elsewhere in what used to be termed the servants' quarters. She was out of sight, but not out of mind. How had she come here? In the refrigerated truck! That was a cert. It would have made better time than our Ethiopian's van. And there had been no body parts for it to transport. Anyway, not Agnes's, of that I was gratefully sure.

A butler wearing a starched white cotton jacket and black trousers passed a first course. Shrimp! That was not a local delicacy, we were too far from any coast. I thought: these shrimp must have been flown in. I thought, "Does that mean there's an airport here?"

The butler was well schooled: he served from the left and removed the used plates from the right. The next dish was roast pork. That indicated my host was definitely not a Moslem. It came accompanied by potatoes swimming in butter, and fresh spinach en branche. Before a new course arrived, a tall cut-glass goblet with frozen sorbet appeared, to whet our appetites. As if mine needed any prodding. Next came a saddle of lamb garnished with sprigs of mint. A trio of desserts followed: vanilla ice cream accompanying chocolate sponge cake and surrounded by fresh sliced peaches.

Conversation had been nil. I was jogged out of my gluttony, when Baku asked: "Coffee, or cappuccino?"

"Coffee, thank you. And then, please I would like to join my children."

"Children? But I understand from Ma Belle that you have no children. Your marriage was barren."

"My husband and I adopted three orphans. They came here yesterday to Chad, with me. Also, I brought my friend Dr. Bruce's three orphans, and Tekla, the nephew of a man who accompanied us."

"Ah. Little African boys. Charming. But they are not in Chad. And neither are you. This is my territory."

I stared at this preening stranger. What could he mean? I remembered we had reached a border crossing. I remembered there'd been a young soldier with a rifle, on duty. I began to feel like Alice in Wonderland. Or perhaps I had gone through Baku's version of C.S. Lewis's closet, only I was in a different kind of Narnia.

This one I sensed was evil.

Why had I been kept in the locked bathroom overnight? To give Baku time to arrive?

So many questions. And the one I'd voiced had been ignored: Baku had not told me what had happened to the seven orphan boys. My three, Ray's three, and Tekla.

"Well, I'd like coffee. Shall we go into the library?" Baku kept up his British lord of the manor act. We progressed into a book-lined room. The books were all leather bound with gold tooling. I read some of the titles: they were in English, all classics: I picked out WUTHERING HEIGHTS, PRIDE AND PREJUDICE, GREAT EXPECTATIONS.

There was American coffee already served in a silver pot. Next to the pot were three large American-size cups. "No demi tasse. I hate small things. Do you like after dinner mints? Of course you do! Ingere, bring Godiva mints."

Ingere, Arabic for hurry up. So, my host employed Arabs.

Interesting! That told me he had no scruples as regarded the Janjaweed, or any other Arabic group that had been slaughtering Sudan's mountain people. Genocidal maniacs were all right in Baku's book, if he had no hang up as regarded the local Arabs.

I expected some conversation at last, over coffee. No. He wanted an audience. Every time I thought to add a remark, he would interrupt with: "And I think…"

Tusk Tooth rejoined us. She smelled of garlic. Baku gestured for her to take the third cup. He said: "I know you don't like the Godiva mints. I'll have Ali serve some Bendicks." Still enjoying his role of generous host, he offered me a cigarette. I declined. I'd been starving, or I wouldn't have eaten his food. I'm not a heavy smoker, I accepted one a week from Lloyd when he was alive. I didn't miss them. But in less fraught circumstances I would most certainly have passed up Baku's food.

Tusk Tooth was not a faithful audience. She made a few unsolicited remarks. "This Ella Phelps, no AIDS. She tested was. I learned. Mahomet arrive tomorrow, other tests will give."

Ali brought in Bendicks chocolate-covered mints: my favorites. Again I declined.

What tests?

While Tusk Tooth munched her chocolate mints, Ali was ordered to take me to my bedroom. Shuddering uncontrollably, I stumbled in his wake. He was fat, dressed in a butler's uniform that was too tight around the middle, and untidily missing a button. He wore Arabs' slippers curled at the ends. I'd noticed the slippers and the missing button because my eyes were downcast. Was I being led to a bridal chamber?

No. I was locked into a clean little room that was simply utilitarian. A camp cot had an added pad with one inch of foam rubber to cover its bare canvas. No chair. But there was a table providing a pitcher of water standing in a large bowl. I stripped and felt the glorious luxury of water bathing my body. There were parts which desperately needed cleaning: my armpits, vulva, and feet. Not to waste this precious water I used what was in the bowl to wash my hair. Glorious. No soap, but I couldn't hope for that. No sheets, no pillow, no pictures, no mirror, only one thin towel.

I fell asleep immediately. Late next morning I was summoned to have breakfast with Baku.

He was outfitted as if to play tennis at Wimbledon, all in white, shorts topped by a designer T-shirt. Was Baku a Christian?

Today he didn't play his role of host very well. He failed to ask how I'd slept, or what I wanted to eat. This time I asked the questions. "Tell me, please: what am I doing here? How long am I to stay? You said I'm not in Chad: where are we? What did you mean by 'my territory?"

Baku lit a cigarette, allowed the smoke to exit his nostrils dragon-style, and smirked: "You are in my part of the Sudan.. You will stay as long as I wish you to stay. You are here as my special guest."

"Thank you for answering me. But I can't stay. I'm responsible for my three orphans, and in fact for the other four I brought with me on the trip you've interrupted."

Baku scowled. He squashed his nearly-new cigarette. "I will show you how beautiful it is here in my territory. Every person owns a piece of property. There are schools for the children. A hospital. A public library. Roads for transport. Many of us have air-conditioning, television, computers. Most importantly, we have ample food. And enough water. I am of the Baqqarah tribe, born near the Al-Arab River, so I know the importance of water for Sudanese people."

"Especially for Moslems, who bathe five times a day." I chanced that remark to find out definitively if he was a Moslem.

Scowling again, Baku evidently detested being interrupted. "I will show you some of our major facilities."

"I'm not a reporter. I can't do a Public Relations job for you by describing what you've done here."

Scowling worse, he continued: "I do not need Public Relations. I am in the oil business. It is doing very well. I have contracts with China which guarantee that our standard of living will continue, and in fact, prosper."

"Do you have a refrigeration plant? At dinner I noticed we had shrimp, and later had some frozen strawberries added to our dessert."

"Not as such. We bring frozen food in our refrigerated trucks. I believe you saw one. Follow me now, and I will show you our tennis courts and my nine-hole golf course."

Was Baku a sports enthusiast? I had taken a more detailed look at his home. There were no valuable pictures, only a few decorative paintings: if a wall was large, there were yards of amateurish dabs of color on the canvas. There was no collection of African carvings, although I did see a stool similar to Laplante's. There were no costly antiques. Baku seemed to favor Danish modern teak tables and uncomfortable angular chairs. I thought it strange that he didn't collect anything of great value in his home.

There was a helicopter on a pad in front of his long low house. It was as dead as an albatross. A fleet of Cadillacs and two Rolls Royces were lined up at one side of his tennis courts. The cars looked as little used as the helicopter.

I wondered if their batteries were charged, with a key in the ignitions, and I could make a run for one of them and drive away. But to where?

Baku turned at the tennis courts and began to climb a high hill behind his house. He beckoned that I should follow. We reached the summit, and I was panting from the effort.

"Do you have a heart problem?" he asked. "I'll see to it that you get an electrocardiogram."

Did he think he was being a kind host! Who would suggest such a test as a gift to a houseguest!

"Thank you, but I don't need one. I'm just not in shape. I haven't climbed any other high hills lately."

For a few moments I stood next to Baku while he pointed out new constructions. I felt as if he was the devil offering me the world, like the scene in the New Testment.

Baku said: "You see that moving cloud of dust on my major road? That means my lab technician has almost arrived at my house. We'd better get back for your tests."

We scrambled down the hillside. I wanted to hold back: I was not eager for any tests. Baku steered my elbow, and once had to catch my hand when I started to fall.

Baku's timing suited him: he arrived at his front door at the same moment that an Arab in a white lab coat entered. They exchanged grim looks and a few sentences in Arabic. I was ushered into a white tiled room that was well fitted for its use as a lab. Baku left us after giving one final order, and I was asked in English by the technician to get horizontal on a metal table.

Electric nodes were fitted at all the necessary points. The test was made. The technician grinned widely. "Your heart fine," he garbled. Next I was sent into a cubicle that had a toilet to give specimens of urine and a bowel movement. Not easy, I hadn't drunk much water except for at last night's dinner. There followed the black band around my upper arm to be blown up like a constricted balloon to take my blood pressure.

The technician listened to my heart with a stethoscope, doubling his grin when that result agreed with the electrocardiogram's. He took a swab from my throat, and peered with the help of a mini-flashlight into my eyes.

Baku returned. Again he exchanged a few sentences with his technician, and matched grins. In English, the technician said: "You not need MRI. I go now." He did not ask for payment. Did Baku have a running account with the man?

I stood lamely in the corridor outside the lab. Baku ignored me and walked with the technician to his Mercedes. While I was on my own, a Sudanese woman arrived on the house steps carrying a huge basket of fresh local fruits. She had seen me standing in the corridor. She wouldn't meet my eyes. No greeting. Why?

Ali re-appeared and herded me back to my cell-like room. I sat down on the camp bed and reviewed the day. Why did Baku show off to me? Why didn't the technician give any gynecological tests? No PAP. No swabs up my vagina. No blood taken. Why?

I wasn't invited to dinner.

A tray with basic food was welcome when it arrived at my locked door, not least because I learned how the lock worked.

I had caught the habit of double chewing to taste twice what was on a plate. That habit made me to think of my orphans, and I spent half the night worrying what could have happened to them.

CHAPTER 11

After two more days of solitude, I was invited again to dinner. Baku was back in his English lord of the manor role. He still did most of the talking, and didn't ask my opinion on anything.

Over coffee, instead of offering after dinner mints, he went to his shelves and took out a thin collection of copybooks. "I think you would enjoy reading this diary," he said. He handed me the collection of copybooks, turned on his battery-operated TV, and dismissed me.

Ali appeared, probably summoned by a hidden electric bell, and I meekly followed him to return to my room.

Alone, I made use of the water in my pitcher giving myself a cat bath, then turned to the copybooks. After finding a comfortable position on my cot bed, I started to read.

The collection's title? JOELY'S DIARY. The pages were yellowed, mildewed and slightly moldy. There was a tired spine, the pages barely held to it. Three generations had passed since it was written between 1930 and 1941, from before during and after the Italian invasion of Ethiopia. It appeared to be the diary of a seventeen-year-old girl who hadn't finished school, and spoke only English in a country where there were many African dialects but where few local people knew any European languages.

The diary began with her arrival in Djibouti, the first stop on a trip inland to Addis Ababa, Ethiopia's capital where her Americanmissionary parents planned to meet her.

I turned to the first copybook, jumbled up with two earlier ones. This one started in the early winter of 1941, when British troops entered Ethiopia in an attempt to oust the occupying Italians and recapture a port that protected the Suez Canal. Winston Churchill had called this fight "a top priority."

Why had Baku lent me this diary?

When dawn sent shafts of pink and mauve in stripes across the far wall of my cell, I took up the 1941 copybook and cheated by sneaking a look at its ending. It had Joely, having collected a group of needy orphans trapped between warring factions, deciding that her best course of action was to reach Addis Ababa with the orphans and find the man she loved. Now I began to truly become involved in Joely's story. Orphans and Africa, and a trek across a war-torn country. Needing to find the man she loved. Yes, that did seem familiar. And yes, it touched my heart.

CHAPTER 12

That ended JOELY'S DIARY. Lucky, because dawn was coming and I needed some sleep.

Breakfast was at noon. Late! Summoned, I took Joely's copybooks to retuen them, and followed Ali through the same corridors.

Baku shoed up at one a.m., and ate his imported American corn flakes silently. When he'd finished his oversized cup of coffee, he growled at me: "I'm going to take you to two of my favorite places. Come along."

Again we climbed a very high hill, this time on the far side of the compound. Above us loomed enormous peaks.

"Marra Mountains," he boomed, adding, "I command most of this area."

"Very big."No use trying to have a conversation.

"The tallest peak is almost seven thousand feet high. We have wonderful birds:geese, cranes, shrikes, and starlings. Sometimes weaver birds."

"Do you shoot gamebirds?"

"Never.I was invited to shoots in England and France.I only enjoyed them when those idiot hunters shot one of their own party. In years past many Europeans came to Africa to kill our animals. Now we have fewer elephants, practically no rhinos, buffalo, lions or giraffes. That disgusts me."

"I noticed that you had no trophy heads of lions or rhinos. Don't you collect anything?"

A weirdly self-satisfied look washed over Baku's face. "Yes. I am a collector of rarities. Just as your English entrepreneurs collect antique furniture or paintings that their ancestors used, I collect what my ancestors liked to collect."

"Can I see?"

"Soon, in my own way, I'll take you to my collection. Look to your left. Are your eyes able to make out an ancient fort? Between it, and my house, I found a former coffee plantation. Coffee grows here on the Marra skirts. We have the right altitude here. Our coffee is about as good as any from Ethiopia.I bought the plantation's facilities when we chased off the coffee pickers after a bad harvest. The owners were glad to give up the facility."

"Glad!"

"Glad to be allowed to save their lives. Certainly, glad. I kept the old copper toasting machine, brought here from

England in 1902. But what I really wanted was its sturdy cement foundation. I had a tunnel drilled underneath, and it's there I keep my collection."

Baku turned, stalked down the high hill and turned me over to Ali.

Although I had only recently eaten breakfast, Ali was carrying a full tray of food as he led me to my room. He handed the tray to me, and order: "Eat."

Why?

Was I to be fattened up like the boy who had to leave the Belgian nuns when he reached puberty? After which he was slaughtered by dealers in body parts!

I caught hold of Ali's arm.He jolted his shoulder to release my hand. I [leaded, "Tell me, are there any boys here?" I was desperate for news of our orphans.

His eyes gleamed strangely. He said nothing, made a noncommittal gesture and headed away down the corridor.

Eating the food, which was roast parridge with potatoes and corn, I choked several times. Afterwards, I kept asking the empty walls of my room: "Felko, and the five others? Tekla? Are they being fattened up? Has Baku a harem of little boys?"

CHAPTER 13

I heard Ray's voice.

It came loud and clear. He was obviously speaking above his usual tone in hopes I could recognize it.

"There is a polio scare here," he said, enunciating very distinctly. "I have had reliable reports of polio cases in this community."

Baku's voice, strained and with loss pomposity, answered: "No polio. I know about you doctors. The United Nations is constantly trying to give me trouble under the excuse we need medical help. Our Sudanese Government has taken your measure. Get out. There's no polio here, and if we get a case I'll fly the person to a decent hospital."

With exaggerated politeness Ray said, "I'm here on another mission. My friend Mrs. Ella Phelps disappeared in this vicinity

I'm here to take her back to our refugee camp, where she has an important job."

"Important? She was washing filthy bandages."

Before Baku could continue, I screamed. And creamed, And screamed some more.

Ray Bruce's footsteps stopped outside my door. Baku switched off the electric lights, but Ray had a flashlight. More importantly, he had a revolver, and fired off two shots. Had he killed Baku? And Ali?

No. Because now I was able to open the door and found both of them nonplussed in the corridor.

The two shots had been fired to free the lock on my door.

Baku returned to his lord of the manor act. "You needn't have destroyed that lock. Ali would have given you the key."

Ray countered, "You have retained Mrs. Phelps here behind a locked door. She will be leaving now. She is going to help me with my vaccination program today."

Baku snapped out: "She had good meals. Water to bathe. Didn't you Mrs. Phelps?"

I didn't answer. I followed the three men down the corridor, my wits in turmoil. Finally, turning to the men I said, "Yes. I ate well.

And could bathe myself. No toilet. A potty had to do."

Maybe I should have kept silent and rationed my dignity. I felt like jumping like a child with a skipping rope when I arrived outside to find two trucks filled with United Nations peacekeepers.

They were Polish, wearing the United Nations uniforms distinguished by their sky-blue berets. These men were standing up in the trucks, packed tightly against one another. Obviously there were more peacekeepers available than trucks.

An officer waved to Ray.

He gave a wave in return, plus a thumbs up signal.

Baku looked on grimly. Ali disappeared.

Arm in arm I went with Ray to a car, hidden behind the trucks. There, a grinning Malaku sat at the wheel.

I rushed to shake hands. "The boys?" I asked. "Your Tekla? Felko? My two others? And, Ray's?"

"Safe. Back at the camp, with the Belgian nun s."

"Agnes?"

"She was home flown to her parents' in Brussels."

Malaku's big grin melted. "News bad is. She venereal disease has.Caught it she from assault."

"Oh!I want to write to her! I'd hoped to be with her when her case goes to trial."

"Trial, no ill happen. Director, he forbid."

Ray opened the car's rear ddoor. "Let's go while we can. I believe I caught Baku off his guard. I know he controls this entire area."

Baku took a stance on his mansion's marble steps. Keeping well away! His posture was that of a guardsman who had been standing like an army scout, watching our get-away. He was glowering like a terrier refused a bone.

Ray gave a signal.Malaku got the car up to speed. The two trucks, so overloaded with Polish peackeepers, followed. Eating our dust.

"Where to?" I asked Ray.

"My job is to vaccinate. At El Caze I finally received a fresh supply of vaccine. I rally have heard of polio near here. I want to put to good use the equipment I brought with me. There's a small city called Al-Junaynah, not far away, with a population of about seventy thousand. There's been a serious outbreak there. These peacekeepers are detailed to escort me."

Malaku added, "Al-Junaynah not far from border with Chad, is. I have friend at border. He tell Dr. Bruce how missing medications go."

That solved one of thequestions thathad plagued Ray.

I said, "Baku, the horrible Baku, boasted that he had an underground facility between the Al-Junaynah fort and this compound where his territory begins. Maybe we should go see that."

"Vaccinations first. Touring, later."

I tried to smile. "It wasn't exactly touring I had in mind. Baku terrified me. I think he has collected something beyond horrible down in that underground facility. I believe he meant for me to end up there. I was being fattened up for slaughter."

Gently, Ray took my hands in his. "We'll check it out."

With the Al-Junaynah fort looming closer, its turrets clearly visible on the horizon, I had a queasy feeling we were driving over Baku's underground facility.

Yes, I noticed the remains of an antique coffee-toasting machine under a large tin roof. The marker!

I pointed. Ray nodded, as did Malaku, the back of his woolly head jolting up and down as he drove. Behind us followed the Polish peackeepers' trucks keeping up with us, like navy destroyers doing a convoy job during World War II.

We stopped at the markers, found an opening to the underground vastness of Baku's collection and made our way inside aided byRay's flashlight. We immediately came on a series of acrylic plinths topped with see-through boxes. With Ray's flashlight's bean zeroing in we could see they all contained body parts of different types. Most of them held scrotum with dried testicles.

I knew that it was an ancient Ethiopian custom to cut off the testicles of an enemy. The custom was supposed to guarantee the enemy would leave no descendants to exact revenge.

On the acrylic plinths were labels naming the originalowners of the body parts. I read the first label, *Haile Galo, Ethiopian, One of two brothers. See box alongside.*

Next to Haile Galos' plinth was one holding a mummified heart. Oh! I could barely force myself to read its label!

Instead of a mere label it had a silver plaque. That read *Lloyd* Phelps, *Eng;ishman.* There was a matching plinth with an empty box, and its plaque read. *Ella Phelps, wife of Engl;ishman.*

I fainted.

When I came to, I was being held by Ray, who had crouched down on the tiled floor to ease my fall.

My God! I HAD been fattened up to provie the heart for that box. Baku had dplanned to have HIS and HERS hearts.

A crazed grunt from behind me alerted that Malaku had recognized an additional line of Amharic writing and now knew that the first plinth's box contained his murdered brother's scrotum and testicles.

He fell to his knees, and prayed, embracing the box as if he was in a church with venerable saint's remains. Finally, he opened the box and with a brief ceremony plucked out the scrotum and testicles to carefully place them in a shirt pocket.'

Baku's collecton of HIS and HERS married couple's hearts and His and Brother's scrotums with testicles were never to be completed. Unlike with Pharaoh Hatsshepsut's liver, which had

remained intact in a box for 3,800 years, these trophies were to be requisitioned.

I couldn't do less than follow Malaku's example. I knelt, said a prayer, and then doefully slipped Lloyd's heart from its horrific perch.

Ray collected it from me with enormous grace, and stored it in a medical tin that he'd found in the bag carrying his polio gear.

Silently we left Baku's ghastly tunnel and climbed back out through its entrance to rejoin our convoy.

When we finally reached the outskirt of Al-Junaynah City, our car slowed down and the trucks behind us followed suit. Ray had a map on his knees and guided Malaku to pass the camel market, from where came the bellows and snorts of the local camels, and w continued on to the city's so-called square.

Long queues of anxious women with their frail children hadformed to reach a tent filled with patients attended by over-taxed nurses and interns. Malaku found a spot nearby, parked the car, and we soon joined the medical team.

Goodbye, Polish peacekeeprs. After waving our thanks, their trucks sped off in more clouds of dust.

Ray was shaking hands with two medicos. He said to me, "This team has ample wherewithal.Syringes, serum, blood if necessary. The team in not giving polio injections. That's up to me."

We took a place in the shade of a tall tree and waited for patients.

They came only too quickly. Dozens of women shouted to be first in line, and one adolescent mother held up an infot for us to see he was already crippled by poliomyelitis.

Ray set up his instruments on a folding table he'd brought. I spread out a sterilized cloth on it and he gestured to the lead patient to enter our circle.

But I wasn't staying.

Ray had involved himself with his patients in such a degree that he didn't notice when I slipped away to find another section of this makeshift hospital.

I went looking for a natal clinic, and found one. "Can I have a pregnancy test here?" I asked.

The answer was "Yes." And after a very quick test, the answer to this was "Yes" again: positive. *I was pregnant.*

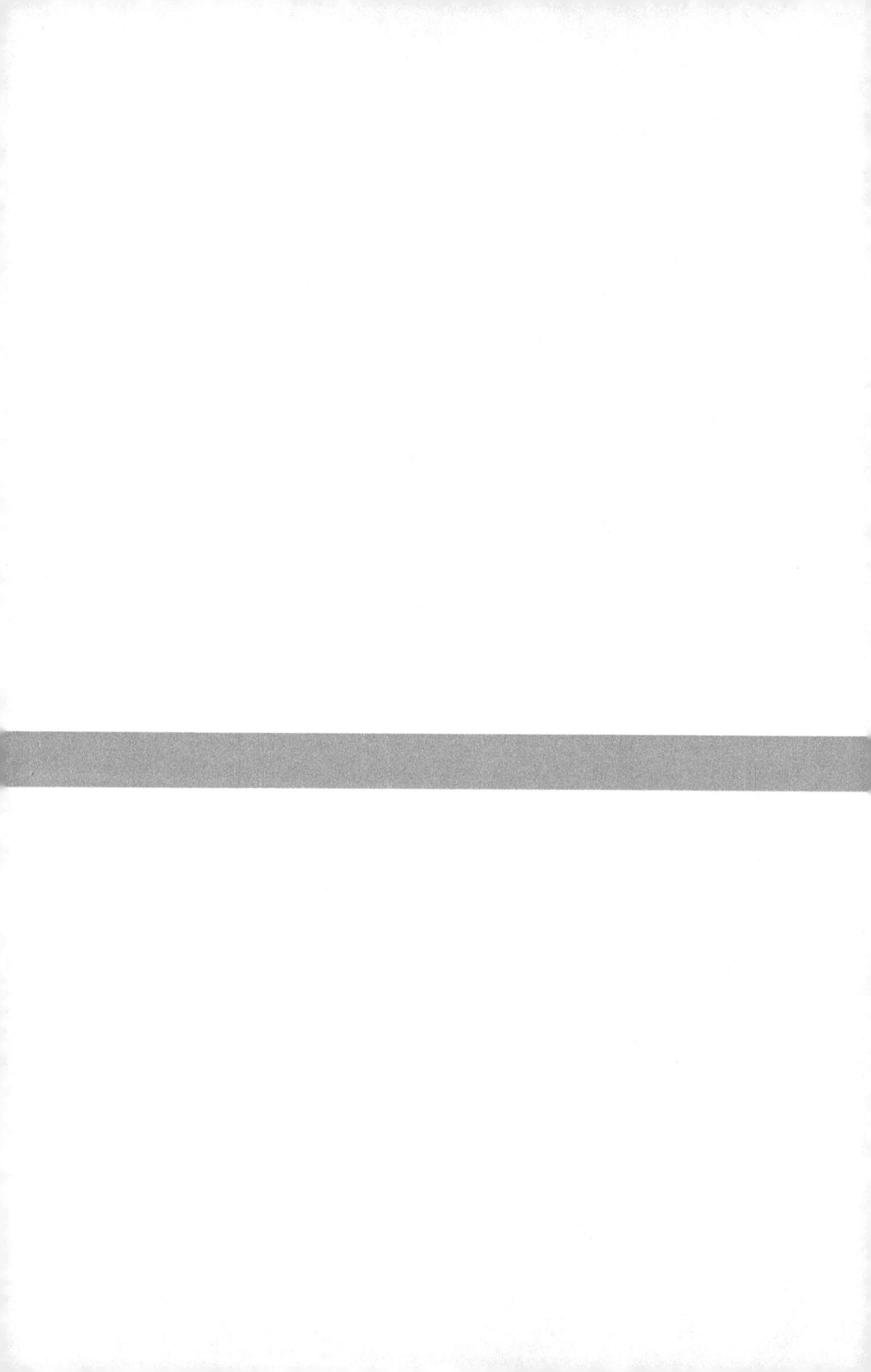

PART TWO

CHAPTER 1

While Ray tended to his avid patients, I slipped beyond his tent and looked for a maternity clinic.

Yes, there was one not too far along the lane. I went inside and asked for a pregnancy test.

Why? Because I'd missed my period, and thought that all those imperious pangs of hunger I'd stifled might have been caused by pregnancy.

This clinic had the fastest result. Glory be, I *was* pregnant. And this baby could only be Ray's!

On a real high from the news of my pregnancy, I failed to notice the arrival of an acquaintance from Newcastle, Professor Alexander Dreyfus, our college's only Nobel Laureate. I really was on a high to miss Professor Dreyfus because *he is big* in so many ways.

He stands six feet four, he weighs as much as a pony, and his physical appearance is quite bizarre. He looks like an affable department store Santa Claus, except that his mouth curves wickedly.He has tufts of white hair surrounding a *bald* pate, his stomach as big as a woman's who is nine months' pregnant with twins, and his feet were the size of a clown's flapping shoes. He speaks in a huge voice, so loud that he never needs a mike to reach the farthest corners of a lecture hall. He has an odd mannerism:his eyes blink constantly. We students called him Blink-Blink.

He called everyone by some qualifying adjective.

I heard that voice before I turned to see him. "Lovely Ella, how wonderful to find you here in Al-Junaynah. I thought you and Princely Phelps were at the Al Caze camp in Darfur!"

I was still on such a high over the news of my pregnancy that I blurted out my news to him. I think I would have grabbed a stranger off the street to tell someone the news if he hadn't been the first person I saw. Didn't I want to shout it from the housetops?

"Professor Dreyfus," I sang out: "I'm pregnant!I've just learned that fact. And, *oh*, it means so much to me after all this time."

Chuckling so hard I thought he'd add a Santa Claus Ho-Ho-Ho, he boomed: "I believe that ladies do like the idea of having babies. Personally, as I've never been married, that ecstasy is one I never shared with a wife. Now tell me all about your work with Princely Phelps. I do know that he's been struggling against the AIDs epidemic, that's rampant in this part of Africa."

Dully, losing the edge off of my happy moment, I said: "Lloyd's been dead over four months. It's almost five months. His heart was ripped out of his dead body and sold to a local warlord. Name of Baku."

"That same Baku I'm here to negotiate with?" Blink-Blink dropped his voice an octave. He frowned like a spinster who has just heard someone fart. "I don't fancy working with a murderer." A huge sigh. "But I do know that it's often necessary in order to achieve one's goal.Remember Prime Minister Neville Chamberlain and his deal with Hitler! Didn't that result in giving Britain time to re-arm?"

Biting my lips, I spat out: "Please don't ask me to deal with Baku."

"Lovely Ella, I was about to ask what you're doing here in Al-Junaynah. And whether you're available to take on a job."

Silence on my part. What a quandary! Here I was in a new country with nine children who needed to be housed, schooled, and fed. Yes, I needed a job. Or did I?

Staring across the cricket field where Ray was still busily working his hypodermics, I asked myself whether he would ask me to marry him and if that would negate any necessity for a job

Ray returned my stare. He and Blink-Blink proceeded to size each other up like two fighting cocks that were about to enter an arena.

Cautiously, not wanting to give away my situation vis-a-vis Ray by a look, I said quietly: "I came here in a car provided by Dr. Bruce, whom you see working with a group fighting polio. We have nine orphans between the two of us, and do what we can for them as a team. I imagine I *will* have to take some sort of job to help feed and house these boys."

"Come, Lovely Ella. Let's cross the field and you will introduce me to this Dr. Bruce."

Ray was not looking his best. The white lab coat was filthy. His shoes had one sole flapping, unsewn. His think hair played wildly in the breeze.

He didn't like any interruptions to his work, and spoke churlishly. "What do you want?"

"This is Professor Alexander Dreyfus, from my university. I took lectures he gave."

Ray didn't stop using his needles. He grunted: "These Sudanese women, they don't believe they've received immunity if you offer the syrup orally. No. It's got to be with a needle."

Blink-Blink, sweating profusely in a tweed jacket and Sherlock Holmes-type tweed cap, totally unsuitable for the African climate, had exerted himself beyond a healthy option by crossing the cricket field. But he retained his worldly manner.

He shook hands with Ray, leaned over the needles and vaccine with an authoritative manner, and said loudly:"Hmm, the IPV. Sanofi Pasteur. Trivalent polio virus vaccine, inactivated, the whole virus grown in monkey kidney cells. Taken by mouth or injected. For virus types 1,2, and 3. For the adults, you want to inject in deltoid area. Each dose should be 0.5 mls. That is,previously unvaccinated persons should have two doses at a one to two month interval and a third one six to twelve months later. Even so, at some point a booster shot should be given." Blink-Blink took a large breath: "Children? Inject in the midlateral thigh. Each dose should be 0.5 ml. But this is not recommended for infants of under six weeks. The full IPV schedule should be one dose at two months, four months, and six to eighteen months. I would recommend sequential schedules of oral polio vaccine for most kids four to six years of age, but never for immuno-compromised patients or patients with immuno-compromised household contacts. Oh, and I would be careful not to offer it when there's hypersensitivity to streptomycin or polymyxin B."

Ray glared at Blink-Blink. He'd been treated like a first year medical student.

I knew that Ray had not only graduated from Imperial College as a biologist, but had worked in the Home Office for input there of his expertise.

Blink-Blink was sparring to win this match by bringing Ray down a level. Ray wasn't having any of that. He grew red like the top of a volcano about to pour lava.

Blink-Blink, very experienced at diffusing anger, said: "Let's the three of us go to my hotel room. Have iced drinks. Maybe a shower?"

I looked at Ray. He nodded, so I nodded. A shower and iced drinks were too much of a bait to resist. As a temp volunteer, he was not bound to stay until the end of the day.

Ray packed up the needles and vaccines, asked another doctor to place them under lock and key, and checked that our orphans were happy playing cricket in a nearby field.

Then we trailed along in Blink-Blink's wake. Going across the wide expanse between the hospital tents and the hotel, we passed by an African dance show. The troupe was as expert as what you'd see at a carnival. The colourful orange, purple and bright yellow costumes sent me thinking of the rainbows I'd seen in my college days on the moors..

The dancers whirled like dervishes. Some turbaned and oddly gowned singers clapped their hands to urge the dancers to perform more outrageously. With my high still in effect, I felt like joining in and dancing their dances. But I didn't. I decided that as a future mother, I should be more discreet.

At Blink-Blink's hotel, a crumbling nineteen-twenties horror with a 2001 façade, we were pushed aside by an over-eager porter. "Sir Alexander, I prepare bath for you?" He beavered away, aiming for baksheesh, bowing and scraping to Blink-Blink, who slipped him a fiver.

Sir Alexander? Blink-Blink had been knighted! Or was the porter merely buttering him up in hopes of still more baksheesh?

Rarely had I seen Blink-Blink look embarrassed. Now he actually blushed. Hoarsely he said: "I got my 'K' just before coming out here.

I imagine Tony Blair had run out of scientists to nominate. But I had a speedy comeuppance. After the investiture at Buckingham Palace, dressed in my morning suit finery, I was standing in Claridge's hallway waiting for a friend, when a woman tourist came up to me and asked me if I knew where the toilets were. She took me for a majordomo."

Ray and I tittered. Politely. That seemed to be expected.

Blink-Blink's room was very basic. But there *was* a small refrigerator. I saw it was well stocked with booze, coca colas and even ginger ale. I'm excessively fond of anything with ginger. I poured out the contents of a can into a glass while asking Ray what he wanted.

"Anything cold. Any rum?'

There was rum. I served Ray. He lingered long over his first sip.

I plunged my hands deep inside the fridge to a basket. It held nuts and crisps. *Glorious!*

Watching us closely, Blink-Blink must have been sizing up my body language and guessed I was in love with Ray. Quietly, he asked: "Anyone for a shower?"Laughing, he added: "Shall we make that a threesome? I need a shower too."

Threesome? No! Not on your nellie. What was that all about? I'd never heard any gossip concerning Blink-Blink. On campus he seemed to be above gossip. Never a word about a live-in girlfriend, or boyfriend. Not a hint that he might be a paedophile, what with all those opportunities for young lads in his lecture halls. But I'm to be part of a threesome?

Ray put paid to that! ""I need a shower too, but I'll defer to Ella. She should be first." He finished off his rum and located another small bottle to add to coca cola.

No waiting around. I quickly found a hotel robe, took it into the bathroom with me, and had wonderful cold water splashing all over my body within seconds. I used the robe to dry myself, because this basic hotel furnished but one towel and I didn't fancy using Blink-Blink's.

As a proper host, Blink-Blink invited Ray to shower next. I think he wanted time alone with me.

His eyes very alert, Blink-Blink asked: "How many months along did you say you are into your pregnancy?"

I hadn't said. There followed a long wait, while I bit my bottom lip and played with the belt of the robe. Finally, I admitted to two months.

"Princely Phelps been dead five months?"

I nodded, while filling up my glass from a second bottle of ginger ale.

"And you've known Dr. Bruce two months?" he bellowed, pointedly staring at the slight bulge pushing my stomach to balloon the robe.

"Yes. Ray's the father." I drew up my chin and stared straight back into those probing eyes. "I love him."

"When is the wedding?" Blink-Blink studied his pink fingernails as if they were more important than the tremendous question he'd asked.

Ray emerged from his shower and into our enclave-of-two. Had he heard? He didn't show any emotion, busily drying himself with Blink-Blink's towel. Was he playing at having gone deaf? Or didn't he want to hear?

I said: "Ray, we'll have to collect the children. No more cricket for today. Not if we hope to find beds for them." Blink-Blink growled:"No rooms for the kids here at my hotel. Place is so crowded I'm told they had to put cots in the corridors upstairs."

Ray smiled. "All's well. I managed to contact my friends the McFees during my break at the tents. They expect us to stay the night. We'll make other arrangements tomorrow."

A knock at the door interrupted further talk of our arrangements. Felko stood there. "Come in I may?" His glance speedily crossed the room to where a cricket bat stood propped against a window. "Is your cricket bat?" He tremulously asked Blink-Blink.

"Yup. Never travel without my lucky bat. Was my magic wand to get me a sports scholarship that propelled me into the great world."

Felko stared at the cricket bat as if it was a loadstone of great power. "Please sir, I may use bat?"

"If you're careful with it, certainly. Tomorrow. Come to see me tomorrow, if you're back in this part of Chad."

I said: "I take it you're not moving to El Caze right away."

"No hurry. Thought I'd look in on the medical facilities at Al-Junaynah first. Glad I did. As I found you, Lovely Ella, here."

I left the room to dress in Blink-Blink's bathroom. I could hear his voice booming away at Ray like a foghorn in a channel warning off boats from dangerous reefs. "Yes, I'm the new Administrator at El Caze. I understand you did a great job filling in for me until Baku caused you to rescue the Lovely Ella.Or were you heading this way in any event in order to contain the polio outbreak here?"

"I came to Africa as a specialist in polio," Ray spoke in his driest tone, not forgetting the put-down of Blink-Blink's extra-long demonstration of what *he* knew about polio vaccines.

Blink-Blink paused before continuing to probe. It was like he wanted to have all his ammunition in place before he said: ""Big problems here in Africa. I've been wondering what the Lovely Ella should do with herself. I read this morning that one hundred died during two days of fighting in the Congo. I learned that through an aid group working in morgues there. Not sure what sparked *that* nasty bit of internecine bloodletting. But I'll wager it had to do with gun-toting by army forces and fighters loyal to their failed presidential candidate Jean-Pierre Bemba. Same sort of thing can happen here again when Baku's men take on Khartoum's Janjaweed."

Ray countered:"The issue here is whether we're building fences or bridges."

"And I agree with that totally. Did you read where our former Prime Minister Tony Blair called the actions of the Sudan Government 'unacceptable!' The German Chancellor, that woman Angela Merkel, called the Darfur region's suffering 'unbearable.' My friend, John Holmes, the new U.N. undersecretary-general for humanitarian affairs, said the aid effort – although it's the largest with its $1 billion budget and some 14,000 aid workers -- was very 'fragile.'"

Ray ignored all of Blink-Blink's newsworthy comments and went to the core."Ella should leave Africa, get away from pestilence and take care of her health."

"Oh, I don't know whether that's really necessary. At school she was always one of the strongest in her classes. I'd like for her to come back to the El Caze camp, and help me while I do *my* job."

"She'd hate that. Her memories of her time there are horrible."

"What alternative have you got to offer her! Marriage, eventually?"

"I hope so."

"Who employs you? What kind of a salary do you have?"

"I work for the First Church of Jesus mission. My salary is none of your business."

"But it could be. If I double it and have you work for me:"

"I'm on a contract. Three more monhs to go. Then I'm free. I hope Ella will marry me then and I'll find other employment. Maybe here in Chad."

"First Church of Jesus mission? I know that lot. Get their money from the religious right in America. Against cell research, against abortion. AGAINST PRE-MARITAL INTERCOURSE: *DIFFICULT TO MARRY ELLA WHILE YOU'RE UNDER CONTRACT TO THEM*!"

How about that? Those two men carving up my life for me!

I charged out of the bathroom like a Miura bull, my head down and if I'd had horns I'd have gored Blink-Blink. Practically spitting, I snarled: "HOW DARE YOU! I'm going o Chad, where I'll get plenty of work to support my orphans."

Blink-Blink reacted as if I'd offered him a box of candy. With a wily smile, he said: "My dear Lovely Ella, have you a visa for Chad? Work papers? I doubt that. And with the enormous amount of refugees competing with Chad's locals, who refuse to be pushed out of the few available jobs, I know you'll have a hard time getting work papers."

"I can find employment in Chad. Right now I'm going downstairs to see the hotel manager to ask him to suggest a – "

As if on cue, stage-managed, a huge explosion rocked the hotel. Stones peppered the windows. One of the room's windowpanes cracked.

Ray tore across the room to shelter me. "Darling, get down on the floor. Stay away from the windows. There may be *another* bomb.""

Bomb!

Our orphans! Were they still playing outside, vulnerable to shrapnel?

Felko had been sipping a coca cola near a window. I crawled on my belly and tried to bring him down to nestle safely beside me, but he wouldn't do that. Instead, he went to the other window, the one that was cracked. He tenderly handled the cricket bat propped there.. It was safe, unharmed.

Blink-Blink had watched this little bit of business and said: "The boy can borrow the bat *now*. I doubt you'll be back here tomorrow. Looks like we're in for a spate of suicide bombings. Better get off to your McFees. I know their address. I'll pick up Lovely Ella there to go on to Camp El Caze, as my Director."

Barely listening to Blink-Blink's amazing offer, I snaked my way into the passage outside his room where I tore down the hallway to rush downstairs.

I went outside to locate my other six boys.

They had all piled into the minibus ready to take us to the McFees' house.

Only Johannus was crying. The other six were fascinated by the carnage in the street alongside their bus. Apparently, they'd been safely ensconced in the bus before the bomb blast.

On the drivers' instructions, the boys had crouched to the floor, but peeked above the seats to watch wide-eyed as heads were blown off, arms and legs sailed through the air, and heads like rugby footballs careened across the playing field.

Patients and doctors in the hospital tents had not been lucky. While I cradled Johannus in my shaking arms, I saw the remnants of white lab jackets spotted with blood, their owners dead on the ground. The nurses' saris were blown off to immodestly reveal their bloodied bare breasts and thighs.

Patients, who'd been in gurneys waiting their chance for medical care, wouldn't be needing cars now. Dead. All dead.

Ray appeared at the minibus door with Felko, who had the cricket bat. "Let's go," he ordered the driver. "There's nothing I can do to help. No injured. All dead. Let's get out of here!"

We had barely reached the perimeter of Al-Junaynah's main plaza when we heard another bomb detonate.

Had Blink-Blink been blown up with all his rash promises of a Director job for me? That carrot, after the stick beating on about me having no visa and work papers for Chad! Plus the insinuation that he'd stop me from getting them.

CHAPTER 2

The McFees were not overjoyed to see us. We'd interrupted their nightly capers.

Mrs. McFee showed some compassion when we told her about the bombing in Al-Junaynah. "Poor souls!"

She ushered the boys to a round hut where there were sleeping cots for a dozen such.

Ray was given bachelor quarters and I was allotted a bare room off their lounge. No food was offered.

I had difficulty going to sleep. My body ached for Ray's, so near and yet so inaccessible. He couldn't have crossed the lounge to me without alerting the McFees. Unfortunately for me, he'd been stopped from doing just that.

When dawn streaked red across the mosquito netting around my bed, I got up in hopes of some kind of food.

Mrs. McFee was already in the kitchen hut. She was preparing a basic meal for about thirty. Would that include my seven orphans, Ray and me?

"Morning." she said brusquely. "This food? It's for the IDP children, the kids separated from their families. Kids who wander on our roads.

The villagers hate them. Say they bring disease, and sometimes steal. One in twenty refugees in Darfur is an IDP, an internally displaced person."

I set about to help her spoon equal amounts of porridge into bowls. But we were interrupted.

Suddenly we heard the trumpeting of elephants. I stared out of the kitchen hut to watch four huge elephants come into the McFees' courtyard and proceed to roll in the dust there. After the rolling, came another show of their joy in finding an open space with plenty of dust. They sucked it up into their trunks and proceeded to spray themselves with the dust as if they were in a shower.

"Good heavens!" I cringed, backing away from the kitchen hut's door.

"Shouldn't fear those elephants. No danger to us if we don't stray into their paths. Not that they couldn't do a lot of damage. Farmers around here complain all the time about elephants eating their crop of bananas or knocking down huts. All that the elephants want is to forage for the food they can't find in a jungle that no longer exists. Or drink the gallons of water they need from rivers that have dried up. These Chad elephants are like the foxes in my native Yorkshire, where foxes have tended to invade private homes for garbage. For the same reason. Their habitat is gone."

I watched the elephants' every move. When they had sprayed themselves sufficiently they simply trundled away in a file like the box cars of an old freight train.

Calmly, Mrs. McFee collected her trays of food and marched toward the empty road.

I followed, eager to help, and eager to see the IDP children.

They hustled toward us like vultures to a carcass. Their hands were terrible. One child was missing a finger: leprosy? Two had bad cases of athlete's foot, bad fungus that caused strips of white dead skin to hang like icicles. All had scabs of one sort or another, some with pus, others with sores that were withering.

Mrs. McFee spoke to them as if they'd arrived with a vicar for tea. In her Yorkshire accent she trilled away knowing perfectly well that these children couldn't understand one word.

I took one of the trays and proceeded to pass its contents to the children. But their hunger was so acute that they couldn't remain politely in line. Like footballers in a scrum, they pushed toward me. Their hands went out grabbing at the paper cups filled withporridge provided by Mrs. Mcfee.The biggest children snatched two or three cups, leaving some of the little ones with none. That's when I strode forward with my tray to personally hand out cups to the youngest.

When all the porridge was gone we distributed tiny little oat cakes that they hid away in their remaining rags. Mrs. McFee held strongly to her tray and motioned for me to return to her compound. The children seemed to want to steal the trays. Perhaps they knew of another town where they could sell them.

Hanging tightly to my tray, I followed her back to the compound.

From the gates I could hear British voices in hot dispute. From the main house, Ray's voice came loudly, arguing.Mr. McFee'sScots' accent was more pronounced than usual when he replied in kind. Both their voices were strident and furious.

"Ach Mon, nay be so selfish. Let the lassie take the wee job. "

"A wee job? To be Director of that cursed camp! Hardly a wee job. She hates the place. Has terrible memories of what happened to Lloyd Phelps."

"Sure, and what's the alternative?

"She can't come with me. There's nothing for her in the areas suffering from polio epidemics. No salaried work for her. And I couldn't expose her to so much disease. She must go back to Newcastle. I can pay for her flight."

"And seven more tickets for the wee orphans? She'll nae go without them!"

Silence. It was as if McFee had made a winning move in a chess game.

I entered the big room and took a stance next to the dinner table. I spooned some porridge into a bowl, took a mouthful of porridge, and said: "Thank you, Mr. McFee, you've clarified my thinking. Yes, I *must* take that job as Director. A great step-up for me, actually. I'll get a nice house for the boys and me. We'll have plenty of money for healthy meals. I might even be able to afford a tutor to give them lessons while I'm at work."

With plenty to say I would have specified more of what I wanted, but there were belching sounds from a large minivan that was coming into the compound. I stared out the window to see Blink-Blink in the front seat with a new driver.

Blink-Blink had changed from his heavy Newcastle tweeds into a 1900's floppy safari hat, and belted jacket. I couldn't make out what else he was wearing until he left the bus. *Short* shorts. Oh! He *did* look a sight in those shorts with his huge belly protruding between belt and shirt.

As if he had overheard my every word, he proceeded to give orders for me to pack up my belongings and the children's. "We are heading for Al Caze now, this morning. And no delay."

Ray, looking abashed, knowing he didn't have anything with which to counter Blink-Blink's offer, interrupted us to bring up the subject of security. "The El Caze camp's very vulnerable. Khartoum's behind the Janjaweed militia, who use the scorched earth policy. They could invade the camp, burn down all the facilities and huts. Who will protect Ella?"

Blink-Blink trumpeted like the lead elephant had this morning. "I'll be right there to see that nothing happens to her."

Ray persisted, "The Janjaweed attack from 4x4s, on horseback, and from camels. Most of them started careers as camel herders and know those animals only too well. They can fire kalishnikovs at full speed from their camels."

"I'll build walls they can't penetrate. Better still, I'll forestall any such attacks by negotiating with the Khartoum Government. I'll make sure the Sudanese President gives orders to the JANJAWEED TO LEAVE MY El Caze camp inviolate."

"I'm afraid that's optimistic thinking.

The President will never contravene the Janjaweed's plans. He's in the pocket of their leaders. Why just the other day he sent Ahmad Harun, his Security Desk Minister, in a helicopter to go with two of the Janjaweed's leaders to gloat with them over the destruction of a town. The town's elders had been corralled, had had kerosene poured over them, and been set on fire. The town's women were raped, and their houses destroyed. All with the object of turning that part of West Darfur into a No-Man's land. By instilling fear, all the men and women abandon a place to become refugees. Eventually the Janjaweed will turn over that area for the government to explore for oil."

Blink-Blink shrugged. "I know all about it. That's precisely why I've come here. To really earn my 'K' and do some good. And I assure you that I will not by any means put Lovely Ella into any kind of jeopardy."

With an imperious gesture he ordered his driver to rev his vehicle. Ray gave me a warm, very caring hug, but no kiss. Not a kiss in front of Blink-Blink!

"Are you coming Lovely Ella? Get yourself and your orphans aboard."

His vehicle burped out gas, we boarded and were too soon away.

Ray's solitary figure stood out against the horizon. He'd remained peering after us like an Apache Indian, erect and grim, until we disappeared.

CHAPTER 3

The camp appeared too soon.

Al Caze looked quite the same as on my first day when I'd arrived as a bride to join Lloyd.

There were no traces of Bernard Laplante, nor of the greedy Director. Gone! "In jail, I've no doubt," explained Blink-Blink. "Sent to a very secure prison in Khartoum, for what I've been told."

Over the following weeks Blink–Blink proved to be quite an experienced Administrator. He demanded a dynamo to have electricity a few hours daily, which meant that he could have his all-important telephone. He delegated control to longtime Darfur refugees who were aware of the camp's main problems. They told him what was needed most urgently: clean drinking water, and wood for carpentry. Every tree for miles around had been downed long ago. The skimpy poles from new growth trees, with their jigsaw piece-shapes, barely managed to hold up the refugees' sheets of plastic that served as roofs.

I needed wood to build bunk beds for my orphans, and a door frame to hold some sort of barrier against hyenas and rats.

Blink-Blink was duly alerted.

Truckloads of wood, and bottled water, promptly arrived at the camp. Adequate salaries went to carpenters, who appeared in droves when told they'd be paid a living wage.

I urged Blink-Blink to stop the incursions of the hyenas. He offered decent salaries to teams who would recover the dead bodies that accumulated daily in our by-way, a great deterrent against hyenas mauling them.

He provided me with Laplante's house. In addition I managed to annex a round hut nearby that Laplante had used to house his servants. Oh yes, Bernard Laplante had been rich enough for servants. You bet!I housed Ray'sorphans and Tekla in the round hut in their freshly-made bunk beds. Each had a clothes pole too, to hang what little clothes they had.

Laplante's former home was my heaven. I put up my orphans in his big bedroom, and kept what had been Ray's for myself. What bliss to lie again on that cot where we'd savored such ecstatic lovemaking.To smell his scent when I opened a drawer where he'd kept his shirts! To find a public hair on a bar of his soap!

The one hundred days marker of my pregnancypassed, so I no longer constantly felt like vomiting or fainting. My stomach was bulging more and more, my breasts felt tender and bigger, but I rejoiced in these symptoms of pregnancy. I had a craving for apples, and Blink-Blink had applesauce sent to me in cans from Khartoum.

The cottage's kitchen was a dream, totally French with such a batterie de cuisine as I'd never seen before. Every possible appliance and gadget was present. There still wasn't much to cook in it, although my salary was sufficient for basic foods. There just wasn't that much in the way of fresh produce in the camp.

All of Blink-Blink's initiatives were not brilliantly successful. Even he couldn't get enough healthy foodstuffs into El Caze. The constant to-and-fro of trucks brought basics, and didn't take away any body parts. But too often the food that was shipped here came rotten or past its consumable date.

And instead of body parts Blink-Blink had to deal with corpses.

In our camp there are so many differentFaiths. The Muslims have to be buried the same die as they die. Christians wanted a Christian burial for family members. The cemetery, where Lloyd lay, had been closed to further burials. Hindus could be burned, but even the so-called hospital didn't have the right facilities to handle quantities of bodies

Blink-Blink surreptitiously sent bodies in trucks on their return trips to Chad, where the authorities there would have to deal with them. Not hygienic!

And there was the Fergus tale. Blink-Blink had speedily kept his promise to hire a tutor to teach my seven boys. Fergus was the tutor's favorite one.

Irish, the tutor spoke with a thick brogue, He had a purple-veined nose that indicated a fondness for booze. His body was slim except for a developing paunch. Too much Guinness, maybe? His hands and feet were small, almost too neat and beautiful, He wore revealing sandals held on by a strap over his one prominent toe. Of course the hair on his head, body and hands was fiery red.

Fergus came with acceptable references. A letter from Trinity College in Dublin recommended him. No graduation diploma: he explained that his had been lost in the many moves that brought him to Darfur.

He taught Latin and Greek to my boys, saying they would need a basic knowledge in those two classics in order to enter the finer schools such as Eton. He endeared himself promptly by refining their cricket skills.

Blink-Blink had provided a space at the edge of the camp for a playing field, in hopes of attracting to it any of the many untutored boys, some of whom might provide at least one opposing team. Our high and mighty Administrator would go to watch his bat being used on that field.

Felko and Fergus soon became fast friends, as close as two fingers on a hand. My problem at first was that Fergus tried to make love to me.

"Oy, and 'tis a most be-*au*-ti-ful day!" he said, brushing a hand over my buttocks as if by mistake, but I knew damn well it was intentional.

He hung around our house, waiting to be fed at mealtimes. He ate like a hog that hadn't been fed in days, except that he didn't grunt. No time given for grunting, just swallowing. He went through our serving platters as if his mouth was a vacuum cleaner. Later, he would open a tired volume of Oscar Wilde plays and poems.

Panting, he would recite: THE GARDEN OF EROS, repeating several times the verse that goes:

"Yon spirited hollyhock red-crocketed

To sway in silent chimes, else must the bee

Its little bellringer , go seek instead.

 Some other pleasance; the anemone

That weeps at daybreak, like a silly girl

Before her love and hardly lets the butterflies unfurletc.etc.etc."

Other evenings he read out: LA BELLA DONNA DELLA MIA MENTE:

"Her little lips, more made to kiss than to cry bitterly for pain

Are tremulous as brook water is,

Or roses after evening rain.

Her neck is like a white melilote

Blushing for pleasure of the sun,

The throbbing of the linnet's throat

Is not so sweet to look upon etc.etc etc."

And there was the early play:THE IMPORTANCE OF BEING EARNEST,with its:

"You behave as if you were married to her already." Fergus would smirk, after that one, knowing full well there would never be any question of marriage for us.

Didn't Fergus realize that as a university graduate I would have read these Oscar Wilde works? Apparently not. Because for some weeks he continued with this ploy.

I thought that perhaps he needed help from Oscar Wilde because his own words were feeble and boring. His breath was awful, and I could hardly stop myself from showing him the door. But I felt I owed it to my boys for them to have a passable tutor.

A scholar? Yet his use of language was dreadful. Oh, he could go on about "the road rising" to meet me, and well-known quotes like that.

I'd had my suspicions of Fergus. But what a conceited fool I was! With my constant talk of Ray, how could I have fallen for his duplicity?

One afternoon I came home early from work. I'd felt odd and thought I'd better lie down. But my cot was occupied by Fergus, a naked Fergus, who had earlier pulled down Felko's trousers and was enticing him to lie beside him.

He stared at me cautiously as I entered the room, jumped off the cot and tried to locate his clothes. Fergus looked horrified that I'd arrived unexpectedly. He pulled up his pants.

It was a terrible scene.

When I could speak, I shouted: "Get out. You filthy pervert!"

He left.Speedily. And when I dragged myself back to the Administrator's office to speak about Fergus to Blink-Blink, Fergus had already collected his salary and quit the camp.

I insisted that Blink-Blink now review the recommendations that had permitted Fergus to take the job as tutor to young boys. There weren't any real ones. He had been expelled from Trinity College for sexually harassing male students. That one letter in our Fergus file had been forged by someone unknown, on paper with the college letterhead.

Oh, how I needed Ray to see what could be done to Fergus and *for* Felko!

Blink-Blink cranked up his army-issue phone and tried to contact Ray at his last known hospital. But Ray had moved on.

I was going to have to face the Felko problem by myself.

First, I took him to our local so-called hospital and had him examined for semen in the anus. Thank God there was none. His anus had not been ripped or damaged.

Felko said: "Mr. Fergus promised to get me a bat all my own, if I would take down my pants and not mention he'd taken down his."

"Has this happened before?

"No, Wozeiro Ella. And will happen not again. Ever!"

I believed Felko, and continued to work fairly happily in my office, although my blissful home was now tainted by the memory of Fergus and his naked body in my cot.But still I could thank God that I'd arrived in time to stopFergus from raping Felko.

Sevenorphans for a paedophile to teach and get close to! What a garden of pristine flowers for that bee to prod with his penis. I'd been so stupid not to have guessed his game. And it had nothing to do with cricket!

Weeks passed and that horrible memory began to fade of Fergus in my cot with Felko. My work proved to be one of the best cures for bad memories.

I immersed myself in the camp's recurring problems. Sewage strewn everywhere. Lack of drinking water. Dead bodies left to rot in the alleys until the hyenas found them.No more space in the Christian cemetery.

I didn't forget to offer help to the Belgian nuns who'd given me hospitality when I'd so sorely needed it. And their orphans.

My dear ever-helpful Sister Agnes was replaced with an equally generous-hearted Sister Aurelie. On my first visit to the nuns' tents she sneaked to me a handful ofalmonds sent to her from her family. Delicious. Healthy!

The new Reverend Mother was difficult. She must have felt she was a law unto herself, and wanted to hold on to her domination of the compound. Other nuns didn't dare speak until spoken to. You'd have thought the place had become a monastery for Trappists who'd taken a vow of silence.

I was invited to eat with the nuns but when I looked in the kitchen and smelled the watery porridge I politely declined and went for a meal with Blink-Blink.

CHAPTER 4

One morning Blink-Blink arrived with a vacuum flask full of hot coffee. He came accompanied by a young woman wearing jockey's boots and jodhpurs, topped with a T-shirt reading GIVE ME YOUR PROBLEMS TO SOLVE. Bling-Bling introduced us, "Meet Mrs. Happy Harrow, a racehorse jockey who's world famous as a sleuth, who volunteered to come here and take a look at the facilities of that damned place where we're going. She was recruited to do this by the United Nations. We're going to take a ride into the other mountains. I need you to come along, and YOU may need this" He poured coffee from his vacuum flask.

After exchanging warm handshakes with Happy Harrow, I accepted a cup of the sizzling delicious coffee, but countered: "No ride in the mountains for me. I don't want to bring on my baby prematurely!'

"Lovely Ella, I'll instruct our driver to take the bumps very slowly, I need you, or I wouldn't ask."

"And what is the destination. Where to, on this drive?" *I had a suspicion I was going to be used, in a dreadful way. Blink-Blink's coffee didn't taste as good now.*

"We're going to see Baku."

"No! You go visit him if you want to. Don't count on me. No way. He's a disgusting monster, and you…"

"Call him a monster if you want to… Call *me* whatever. Sorry, Lovely Ella. But this trip is essential. You go with me, or you're fired."

Fired? With nine mouths to feed, counting my orphans, myself and the baby inside? Who would employ a four months' pregnant woman, unmarried, and with seven orphans?

Silently, I tidied my desk, taking a long time about it. But eventually I followed Blink-Blink and his jockey friend to get outside and into a luxurious Mercedes Benz that had been provided us.

"We have to put on a good show for Baku. " Blink-Blink said, pointing at the car. "Can't let him out-shine us."

"Bloody hell, as if he could!" I snapped bitterly, as the limousine started its long horrid bumpy journey.

That was the end of any so-called talk between us. I started to tremble, at first quite gently but in ever-increasing spasms as we approached Baku's plateau. Oh, how dreadful it was to drive over the spot where Lloyd's heart had been encased. Worse, to approach Baku's splendiferous mansion.

CHAPTER 5

Baku was waiting for us on the marble stairway, in his Lord Of The Manor pose.

What with my intense trembling, I could barely manage to leave the car. I shrugged off the helpful hand that Blink-Blink offered. I climbed the steps, ignoring Baku. Oh! What a penance to have to enter his doorway again.

My legs gave way before I reached the vast hallway.

Baku's servant Ali, in a gold-braided tunic over purple ballooned trousers, rushed forward.

Ali dragged a throne-like chair to me and helped me into it. I felt terrifically dizzy still, and wanted desperately to go pee.

Instead, I sat quietly while two of Baku's farmer-soldiers appeared, wearing white jackets over black trousers fitted to make them look like household servants, and carrying two buckets of ICED champagne. We were served it in crystal Baccarat goblets, accompanied with nuts and hot hors d'oeuvres.

Negotiation time.

Blink-Blink first introduced a carrot. "Sir Baku," he began by giving the bandit a title equal to his own, "I have a great plan for this area: my sponsors will build a hotel here. You have the road, and a helicopter pad. Hotel rooms are desperately needed."

"What? And have every penniless lout move here?"

"I assure you that would not be the case. Journalists, government people, UN officials will use the rooms. Suites, if you prefer. Some of the newer hotels offer suites only."

Sullenly, Baku grabbed a leader's role. "I'll think about it. But really, I haven't any suitable space for such a facility. It would need basements, garages or parking lots. And air-conditioning – "

In a weak, low voice, I interrupted: "Yes, Mr. Baku. You most certainly DO have the space." Ready to vomit again, I managed to add:"Where you keep your COLLECTION."

A deep silence!

Now Blink-Blink introduced The Big Stick. "In March 2007, in the USA, a federal district judge, Robert Doumar, ruled that the Sudanese government caused the terrorist bombing of the USS Cole and will be liable for paying damages to the families of the seventeen sailors killed in that attack. You'll recall the case: the USS Cole was in Yemen's port of Aden when on October 1st, an explosion ripped a 40-foot hole in its body. You want to be included with the Sudanese government to pay those damages?"

Bulls-eye! Blink-Blink hit his target. Baku was the one blinking now.

First the carrot, then The Big Stick. God knows Blink-Blink used that ploy on me.

Baku growled: "I'm not aligned with the government. Not with its Janjaweed. I'm not going to be liable for damages. What? A million dollars for each dead sailor? You *can* HAVE your damned hotel!"

Smiling with satisfaction, Blink-Blink rose to leave.

"Wait! I have a banquet prepared for you."

We watched as the two servant-farmers opened the dining room doors. A buffet table was spread with slices of cold fish, a roast leg of beef, and Jersey potatoes accompanied by a huge assortment of local produce. I thought: "Maybe the fish is just Nile perch, or it could have been flown in frozen from God knows where. But the leg of lamb? I know damn well in which refrigerated truck THAT could have arrived in." And I vomited, right there all over Baku's white linens and polished silver, like President George Bush had done, vomiting over his host art a banquet in Tokyo.

Ali held me erect by my forehead to stop me from falling into my vomit. The two white-jacketed servants, like Darfur's hyenas in the role of garbage men, rushed away to return with damp cloths to wipe up the vomit.

Blink-Blink shrugged at the embarrassing end to his negotiation with Baku. But Blink-Blink had achieved what he'd come here to get and so he overlooked the mess. He waited until I'd finished vomiting, then took my free arm and led me back to his borrowed Mercedes Benz. He finally paid attention to Mrs. Happy Harrow. "Did you get enough information today to get action against Baku from the UN? You may not be an officially named Ambassador for the UN, but I do know you've got plenty of clout there."

Modestly, not preening herself at all, this ultra-quiet woman nodded. "Ah done looked into his ledgers." She had a very noticeable Kentucky Hills accent. Her eyes were bright, and she exuded knowledge.

That was a bonus I needed to see.

WITH A NOD FROM Happy Harrow, this episode was terminated. Thank God it was over.

Blink-Blink demonstrated his humanity by *not* returning me to El Caze, but ordering our driver to take me to that same mediocre hotel in Iriba where he'd first become a so-called friend by offering me peanuts, crisps, and a shower.

All seven of my dear orphans were already out in the Iriba hotel's grounds making use of Blink-Blink's cricket bat. Felko was ordering them to play like the team leader he hoped to become. Blink-Blink had interrupted their studies at El Caze and had them transported here for my delight.

Wonder of wonders, I was given a room of my own at the hotel for R and R.

I fell asleep immediately, to dream of Ray Bruce. In my dream he was kissing me softly on the forehead. No sex in the dream, just sweetness and caring.

CHAPTER 6

I woke to find Blink-Blink staring at me from a chair opposite my bed. He'd created a mini-cathedral nave by cocking his fingers and he was observing me through the tunnel of fingers. I sat up quickly. I didn't like being in "a state of undress" in front of Blink-Blink. How had he got into my room anyway? I'd locked the door.

Even though I'd admired the way he'd used the carrot-and-stick method to win over Baku, I still wasn't confident about his behavior as a male.

He said brusquely: "Good! You're awake. Lovely Ella, I've something to tell you. Because you faced up to Beastly Baku and caught him out so that he had to agree to let us use his Collections' facility, I've gone to bat for your boys. I've made arrangements for six of them to leave Africa."

Arrangements? How dare he meddle in the lives of our orphans?

Tekla, Ray's and my orphans were not HIS to play God with.

I was angry and so I snarled at him: "IT'S NOT UP TO YOU TO MAKE ARRANGEMENTS FOR THE BOYS."

Blink-Blink took no notice of my fury. Like a bishop in a pulpit, he sounded totally confident in the righteousness of his deeds. "I've made telephone calls to England and found places for all the boys. Felko has a cricket scholarship at a public school, where the powers that be have always liked to have an African in the student body. I couldn't get a cricket scholarship for Mircke because he doesn't play well enough. But I heard him sing LONDON BRIDGE IS FALLING DOWN, and as he has a most marvelous voice with those spectacular and rare high notes so beloved of English choirs, I got him into the Westminster Choir School. As for Tekla, since his uncle is now out of hospital, I was able to get him to agree that Tekla goes to the Ethiopian monastery in Jerusalem."

I hesitated to ask what arrangements had been made for Ray's three orphans.

But I did.

"Brave Dr. Bruce's boys? I reached the good doctor's brother, he took two boys and the other one goes to a sister. They may have difficulty acclimatizing to those fierce Scottish winters, but other Africans have managed. As I recall, Sir Frances Dunsany kept an African page always. Dressed like a blackamoor, in satin robes and a turban."

I shivered.

How was it that our little family could disintegrate so fast?

Feeling remorse for my disinterest in Ray's family background. I blushed to realize I had never asked about Ray's family: I hadn't bothered to delve for the facts that he had a brother and sister in Scotland. I hadn't asked. What were their names? How old were they? Were they married, and with children of their own? Did he have a mother and father alive? God, I'd been using Ray as a stud, without regard for what other areas of his heart were spoken for.

When would I see Ray again? There could be no hope of his returning to Chad so long as polio continued to sweep through Darfur.

In as polite a tone as I could summon, I said to Blink-Blink: "Please leave my room. I'm going to get dressed and see how my boys feel about all of your arrangements."

As very often lately, I found all the boys were playing cricket under Felko's tutelage. None were pleased to be called out of the game to answer questions. Only Johannus, who had been spared an "arrangement," came running to join me and cuddled his way into my lap. Blink-Blink must have realized that Johannus still needed me as a surrogate mother.

When I stopped a waiter and ordered cokes for the boys on Blink-Blink's bar bill, they crowded around once the cans appeared. They had very quickly discovered a taste for coca cola. Would they as quickly acquire a taste for cold England or freezing Scotland?

"Felko, has Sir Alexander told you that you've been given a cricket scholarship at a school in England? Are you happy about that?"

"Yes, Wozeiro Ella. Happy I am. if he his cricket bat gives me."

Oh! So much for all the mothering I did for Felko. "And Mickey the Mouse, will you be happy singing with a choir in London?"

"I know not, Mrs. Ella. High notes I cannot always reach."

Mickey the Mouse looked worried. His fat lips were turned down. What would happen to him in a few years' time when his voice changed as he entered puberty? What welcome would London offer him then!

Ray's three boys seemed excited over the prospect of going to Scotland. I remember having listened while Ray spoke to them in the van's journey and described Scottish wildlife: the ferrets, the grouse, the rare ptarmigan. Would his brother or sister take the boys to shoot game?

Tekla was decidedly unhappy about the prospect of living with Ethiopian monks in Jerusalem. When Tekla lived in Ethiopia few monks remained there because during the Red Terror all the monks had been pressed into the army. Their Bibles and holy pictures were sold by the bushel in bazaars all over Africa. Except in Ethiopia. Forbidden there!

The only monks who avoided military service were unassailable due to their remote locations such as those in a monastery on a mountaintop reached only by an unreliable rope.

I didn't think that Tekla had ever seen or met a monk. "Mrs. Ella," he moaned: "Jerusalem I know of, from lessons of Bible you gave. Monks? I know not of monks. What food eat they?"

Tekla had never been as greedy for dinner as Mircke and Johannus, but he could wield a mighty fork just the same. How could I answer? I'd no idea what food or quantities of samethe Jerusalem-based monks would provide. I guessed it would be very different fare from our African roots and fruits. Not that any of those had been plentiful on our dinner table. But Tekla'd grown happy with what we'd had. Good God, what do Ethiopian monks in Jerusalem eat anyway?

Blink-Blink demonstrated his know-how with boys from his many years as a teacher: "Hello, chaps," he said cheerily, with his tummy fat wobbling from the effort of rushing across the cricket pitch. "I've ordered some meat patties from the hotel kitchen for all of you. Will you join me on the hotel terrace?"

No argument from the boys. They'd quickly learned that Blink-Blink's offerings of food were generous and usually delicious.

Why the hotel terrace?

I soon found out.

RAY stood there, quietly, self-effacing and with a yearning expression. He rushed to join me and kissed me in front of Blink-Blink and the boys.

It wasn't all bliss on the terrace. Yes, I revelled in being reunited with my man. I'd savoured that kiss as if it was ambrosia OF THE GODS. I felt grateful to Blink-Blink for arranging this wonder, but *what about his other arrangements?*

Blink-Blink quickly filled me in on why he'd brought Ray here. "I'll need Brave Dr. Bruce's signature in order to get British visas for his tree orphans. Both his brother and sister have already sent ahead the particulars necessary for having them go to Scotland. Now, Lovely Ella, I need your signature regarding Felko and Mircke."

Ray placed his arms around me protectively as if we were experiencing the fallout from a suicide bomber's devastation.

I wanted Ray's penis in my vagina.

Blink-Blink must have had some understanding of that because he showed another facet to his personality by saying: "You can have my room at the hotel. I have to get back to El Caze. Your orphans can be housed in what was the hospital before that suicide bomber destroyed most of it two months ago."

"Is the building safe?"

"What *is* safe? As long as the would-be suicide bombers are promised $15,000 to their families in exchange for blowing themselves up, no, not many buildings anywhere are safe. I hear that in Iraq's Green Zone there have recently been bombs."

"I guess I've just got to pray for my boys' safety. And the hospital does have strong walls. They withstood the bombing here."

"They did. It was the people in the tents who died. No injuries inside the building."

The tents! I thought back to the sight of Ray vaccinating children

in one of those tents. My Ray! If I hadn't bumped into that rascally old professor, Blink-Blink that day, it could have been my baby's father who had been slaughtered. Those severed heads feet and hands I'd seen could have been RAY's.

Sweet little Johannus interrupted that horrific thought. He objected to any separation. "Mrs. Ella I want with you stay."

Difficult to sidestep his plea. I murmured: "You must be with the other boys as long as you can. They are leaving us for a long time .And you'll be missing them."

Remembering what a glutton my little Johannus was for any kind of food, I rummaged in my bag for a piece of candy, which I made much of at placing it on the pillow of the nearest bed. Johannus went straight to the candy. I tucked him between the crisp new sheets, and kissed all the boys goodnight.

As kindly as I could manage, I disappeared with Ray.

Blink-Blink's room was a marvel when we had it all to ourselves. It had a new Queen-sized bed. There were sturdy shutters on the two windows for privacy – but also for safety, the shutters added since the devastating bombing.

Copying European hotels, the bathroom now had an assortment of treats: body creams, shampoo, sample size perfumes and even a deodorant. I used everything.

Ray had arrived with K-Y. Naughty man. I guess he felt very sure we'd make love this time somehow, somewhere.

And make glorious love we did. For three nights. What stupendous lovemaking. Ray was very gentle with me and careful of our baby nestling inside my tummy. But we were imaginative. Until I was so tired that I drifted in and out of sleep. Even then Ray's imaginative caresses were all I needed to start responding again.

The days were awful. In addition to the emotionally-searing prospect of losing the orphans, we had never ending difficulties trying to make the necessary arrangements for their departures. Our hotel *did* offer e-mail and FAX, but these contemporary boons were not sufficient to pacify nosy bureaucrats.

"You may have to take the boys to Khartoum. They are citizens of the Sudan, and you have a visa for Sudan."

Malaku had reappeared on our first day, quite recuperated, and eager to take away his Tekla. So our Ethiopian was able to abscond with his blood uncle, and escape Blink-Blink's plan to send him to the Ethiopian monastery in Jerusalem. They left us to go back to El Caze, to finalize the reburial of his brother's body parts that he'd recuperated from Baku's horrific collection.

Ray financed our flights to Khartoum. He stayed behind, because he'd received an urgent message from McFee to come to their compound where polio was now rampant.

In a pathetically-worded aside, McFee had alerted Ray that his wife was afflicted.

Kindly Mrs. McFee would have caught polio from those IDP children she fed. Those children had brought polio to the village, just as its villagers had predicted.

CHAPTER 8

Khartoum! What an experience to arrive in an airport that was ccupied mostly by armed troops carrying kulishnikovs, and as silent as if all the would-be passengers were prisoners in a gulag!

Frightened faces matched their silent tongues as they filed to counters where girls in the Muslim's favourite green dispatched tickets without the merest smile.

Driving by bus into the city, I felt as startled as my children to see high-rise buildings and hear the screeching of traffic.

Much of the traffic consisted of army trucks filled with heavily armed soldiers wearing khaki uniforms topped with black berets. They looked like the photographs of Janjaweed men I'd seen.

"We'll be safe enough in our hotel," I promised the children.

The hotel was seedy and sad. Its ill-kempt façade of peeling paint didn't promise a cheerful interior. Our rooms were disgusting. The bathroom we shared hadn't been cleaned for God knows how long. There was a Muslim woman's discarded naquib in the brown-stained bidet. I'll bet that the bidet had been used as a toilet by savages from the hills who'd never seen one and didn't know what its purpose was.

I was reluctant to explain its proper use to my boys. As soon as they'd freshened up to look presentable for the British Embassy, I marched them there. We were on a very tiny budget and could not afford the luxury of an inter-city bus.

Little Johannus complained non-stop.He didn't need to go to the embassy but would not be left behind alone at the hotel

"Is too far. I tired am."

The bureaucrats at the embassy were atrocious. They acted so superior to us, although most of the staff had been recruited locally and were Sudanese.

In an arrogant tone, the first woman was so condescending I wanted to kick her:"And you think these children are acceptable immigrants to the United Kingdom!" she bit out."You know what they do to African boys in London? Just the other day one of them was killed and his torso thrown into the Thames. Killed for Voodoo, in Central London."

Very scared, Johannus began to cry. I kept a stiff upper lip and changed the subject rapidly. I coolly suggested to the woman that the father of three of the boys has a brother in Scotland who will explain all to her. I'd arrived with a primed mobile telephone bought on our long, long walk. I dialled Ray's brother, introduced myself, and pleaded with him to speak to the detestable woman. At least she didn't refuse to speak to him on the telephone.

Ray's brother was wonderful. Whatever he said to that woman, she melted and began to hand out forms for the boys to fill. They needed my help, but all of them could read well enough to do what was necessary.

I was summoned into a boyish flunkey's office, who was self-effacing and polite. He ripped my heart apart by asking me to release my rights to Felko and Mircke. Which I duly did, with the most tearing emotion.

Two days and nights in Khartoum.

I couldn't sleep. I hated the food in the hotel that was included as bed and board, but we didn't have enough money to try a decent restaurant. Johannus, of course, finished off whatever was left on our plates.

On the evening of the second day I had the horrible duty of seeing off all the boys except Johannus. Their flight to England was late, and we had to sit in that grotesquely silent airport with no money for food, drink or entertainment. I wept. The boys tried to comfort me, but there was no stopping my tears.

When their flight was finally called, it was Johannus who stood like a stalwart knight to put his little arms around me as the boys filed past the entrance to duty-free. I was not permitted to follow. The last I saw of any of them was a vignette of Felko, peering longingly at a cricket bat in the airport's sports shop. He was so magnetized by that cricket bat that he forgot to wave goodbye.

Careful not to place my sorrow on Johannus, I didn't invite him to sleep in my bed. No, I'd read somewhere that it wasn't healthy for a seven-year-old boy to share a bed with a woman. Although Johannus was such a *little* seven year old!

CHAPTER 9

We didn't return to Iriba. An urgent message from Blink-Blink demanded I go straight to El Caze.

What a trip! I could swear that most of the other traffic on the roads into Darfur was by the Sudan Government's army trucks loaded with JANJAWEED SOLDIERS. There was no food on our bus. Johannus kept asking when we'd eat. I *had* made up sandwiches from the breakfast bread and jam provided free at our hotel. He ate every crumb which left nothing for me. Anyway I felt like vomiting for most of the bumpy trip. My need was for water.

Ray was standing at the bus platform when we arrived. He'd thoughtfully brought cakes and my favourite brand of ginger ale, not iced, but so delicious after so many hours without anything wet.

"Ray! My darling! What are you doing in El Caze? I thought you'd been summoned to the McFees'."

"His wife is dead and he's in a miserable state. I vaccinated all the villagers who were not ill. Tricky, for the ones who'd been exposed to a patient at home. But you know about that. Blink-Blink explained how that works when he lectured me like I was a first year med student."

"Oh, but I'm so glad you're here! Awfully sorry, of course about that dear Mrs. McFee. She'd come to Africa to do good and Africa killed her.

Ray!" Suddenly I felt scared for my Johannus. "Is there polio here at El Caze? Is that why you've come?"

"Yes. You guessed it in one. A few cases. But it's spreading. The IDP children, who wander homeless on the roads, brought polio to El Caze. Like AIDS, it's often the people on the roads who bring disease to village after village."

"Oh my God! I don't know whether Johannus had been vaccinated before he came to me."

"And you, precious Ella, have *you* been vaccinated?" Ray's voice dropped an octave for that question.

Walking together toward the Laplante cottage, I sent my thoughts back to the day in school when all of us girls received the old time Salk vaccine, from when it was popular in the 1980s. "Yes. With the Salk."

"Ella, you should have a booster with the newer vaccine, one I do believe works against *this* particular strain of the disease."

No argument. I wanted to be vaccinated in front of Johannus, to ease any fears he might have of a hypodermic needle. Johannus, a hyperactive child who needs too much food to calm his nerves, was liable to be scared.

Ray had already set out all that was needed on a white cloth on the dining table. He must have resolved we'd need booster shots before he'd asked about our med history.

I'd had my needle, and Ray was about to inject vaccine into Johannus who had his eyes tightly closed, when a determined rapping almost broke the cottage's door. Letting go of his hand, I left Johannus to Ray, and opened the door.

Near hysteria, Malaku stood there, weeping. His hands still played a loud tattoo on the door as if he needed that to help him through his present agony.

"Malaku, dear Malaku! What in heavens' …?"

Choking through his torrents of tears, Malaku groaned: "Wozeiro Ella, Tekla, he dead."

Ray swabbed Johannus's arm, and crossed to the threshold. "Polio?"

Malaku nodded woefully. He stopped the tattoo on the door, but grabbed my free hand and squeezed like a gardener emptying a hose.

With an understanding grimace, Ray urged Malaku to come inside. He found where I kept the beer, and served one to Malaku. "Drink it!"

"No place in Christian cemetery is there. Cemetery closed to burials new."

Trying to ease Malaku's misery, I murmured: "I can arrange for him to be placed next to his father's retrieved body parts. They had a proper burial."

Malaku released my hand. "Wozeiro Ella, how he die quick like?"

Ray answered that. "This strain of the virus hits fast and kills fast." After a pause, he asked: "Malaku, have you been vaccinated?"

Shaking his head Malaku uttered through his groans: "I die should. No one left in family."

Not dignifying the last comment, Ray walked to the clean white cloth, tore open the cover of a hypodermic needle and proceeded to fill it with serum.He plunged it into Malaku's arm without further questioning.

Johannus piped up: "Does not hurt too much. I *very* brave was, with needle."

My mobile phone rang. I answered.Blink-Blink spoke in a strangled tone at the other end. "Come quickly. But avoid the main square," he ordered.

Ray had overheard. "I'll come too."

"And me shall come." Malaku left the stool where he had collapsed after the needle had worsened his tragic mood.

We left Johannus in the cottage. When last I looked, he was quite happily chewing on nuts from a bowl.

Of course I went straight to the main square in direct contradiction to Blink-Blink's cautionary order.

Ray and Malaku, neither protesting, followed.

In the square, under the vast shade tree where the sabre-toothed hag had once held sway, there were two trucks filled with Sudanese government soldiers wearing their khakis and black berets. They were well-armed with machine guns and mortars.

None of the soldiers had on a helmet, presumably because the soldiers expected no armed resistance.

I drew back, out of sight. Any soldier could have found me by searching through the telescopic lens of a rifle. None did.

"Let's go to Blink-Blink's office," I breathed.

"On the double!" Ray agreed.

We two dashed away in the direction of the office.

Malaku remained behind. "I learn more this day of trucks."

Impossible to dissuade him!

Blink-Blink had lost his Ivory Tower calm. In a rage he roared at me as I walked into his office, panting from running, my huge stomach carrying me forward like a ship in a southwesterly gale.

"What took you so long. I need your mobile phone. The dynamo's been cut off. No electricity, no phone. At least not the kind I've been using."

I gasped: "I don't know how much longer mine will work. I haven't been able to juice it since Khartoum. I bought the only one in the shop that *was* juiced up."

"Don't waste my time in talk. Hand me the phone. I've got to call Baku."

"Baku!" Ray and I repeated that name together.

"Who else has the manpower to stop the Janjaweed from taking over this camp!"

Feeling stupid, because in our main square I'd seen those two trucks filled with Khartoum's soldiers, I echoed: "Janjaweed."

Ray growled. "Surely Baku's behind this Janjaweed invasion,"

"Not at all! One of Khartoum's men, a nasty piece of work," Blink-Blink interrupted himself to take my phone and dial Baku's number: "a sleeper,planted here to eavesdrop on my conversations, learned that we've had a geologist confirm there are valuable mineral deposits under the camp. After all, I *am* a specialist in – *Am I speaking to Sir Baku personally? Yes, I need you and your men urgently. As we discussed, you will not be prosecuted if you aid us. Bring your helicopter. Armed. At once. Speed up your men to arrive soonest.*"

My mobile was fading, I could tell that because it was beeping loudly asking for juice. I retrieved the useless phone, and shouted: "Johannus! He's alone in my cottage. Trucks are sure to use the road outside. He'll be right in the midst of any fighting." Holding my tummy with both hands for ballast, I leaped out of the office and headed for home.

Behind me, I heard Ray questioning: "Mineral deposits?"

CHAPTER 10

Johannnus was seated at the dinner table still picking at the bottom level of nuts from the bowl. His inner cheeks were fat with them.

"Mrs. Ella, many trucks pass have they. You hear rumbling of trucks?"

"Yes, dear. But let me make you some supper, and then it's sleepy time."

"Trucks, I like. Big ones, small too. In Iriba saw trucks carry earth."

"Yes, dear. What would you like for supper?"

"Meat!"

"I'm afraid we haven't any for tonight. But I could fry bananas, make rice."

Disappointed, Johannnus nevertheless went to the cupboard for his dish and a fork.

At that moment the cottage shook from a mortar blast. I threw myself over Johannnus, my huge stomach covering him like a turtle's back.

He began to cry.

My! But Johannnus really is a most overly sensitive child.

Recalling what I'd read in JOELY'S DIARY when sequestered at Baku's, I decided to put some steel in my back and take decisive action.

"Johannnus! Come along, we're leaving here. Follow me!"

"Can I take the bananas?"

I threw three bananas into my bag and we dashed out into an alley that led away from the main road.

Mortar fire continued to blast away, but the fragile plastic tent homes didn't even shiver because there was no foundation to move them. But their people oozed out of the houses like condensed milk from cans. Mortars, yes, but I could also recognize kulishnikovs and some Chinese manufactured guns raised by the invading Janjaweed.

The Janjaweed had invaded all our byways. The government trucks that had deposited those few soldiers earlier had been only the forerunners for this massive push. Mounted on their camels, the Janajaweed were penetrating every trail I tried. Like a melting glacier, theypoured into every opening in the camp.

Looking dazed, or terrified, or merely dysfunctional the children from the houses joined me and Johannus. The adults, more knowledgeable of what those mortars could mean, prepared to leave with what possessions they could carry. And my friendly Belgian nuns: where were they? Their tents were in the line of fire, but I didn't see them join the ant-like lines of refugees.

Soon there was a line snaking away from the main road. Most people had loaded their belongings on their backs like beetles after a find of sweets.

Caught in this tidal wave of humanity, I couldn't get far with Johannus and the children of my neighbours. The fact that I was so heavily pregnant didn't dissuade anybody from giving me a push when there was an opening ahead.

Walking slowly or rushing or being stopped made little difference. Overhead we heard a helicopter. Baku's?

Funny, when last I'd seen Baku's helicopter the day we escaped to Chad it caused very different feelings from today. Now I hoped it *would* be Baku's, coming to fight for us.

I well knew that our alley led to an open clearing where we would all be vulnerable to any crossfire. Hurrying Johannus, I tripped once, and it turned out to be a lucky thing I did.

By tripping I was held back. But sadly I watched a horrible scene as dozens of children were mowed down by machine gun fire. They could have been nothing more than grass to a harvester the way the bullets brought them down. Horrible!

Clutching Johannus to me, who was too tired to walk any farther, I held him to my enormous belly like a mother kangaroo hides her baby in her pouch.

But a Janjaweed soldier had spotted a white woman prey. I saw him swing his rifle in my direction. There was no chance to duck.

I felt a shove. I heard a bullet enter flesh. I turned: Maliku had followed us and come in time to see the shooter aim. He'd taken the bullet.

There was a gaping hole in his chest. Blood spurted in the way it does when a major artery is hit. He gasped: "Go. Wait not." A gurgling sound followed, then the death rattle.

I knew there was nothing I could do for Malaku. I covered his dear face with my shawl and rushed away. In a few yards I spotted a sturdy round hut, a tirkal-shaped one that indicated it had been built long ago before this region ran out of reeds. I urged Johannus to go inside, and after a pause I went in too.

A Muslim woman crouched in terror in one corner. I said in my broken Swahili: "Please, give us hospitality."

The woman nodded. She'd got a long peek at my big tummy. That, and because according to Muslim custom once a traveller enters your home you are bound to offer hospitality, she kept nodding.

Without a word she left her corner, grabbed a yashmak and a djellabah, and dressed me in them. She ran her fingers over the dirt floor and painted the small visible area around my eyes with earth. She well knew that as a foreigner and a white woman I was in jeopardy.

I thanked my God that He was also the God of Muslims. As this home belonged topeople who were on the side of the Muslim Janjaweed, it was unlikely they would be victims in this conflict.

There was one hiccup when my mobile phone began to beep, asking for its electrical juice. Our Muslim hostess looked positively terrified, knowing that its beeping could draw attention to her tirkal. That didn't happen.

Johannus and I remained safely in her home until the fighting ceased. There had been lulls, and then shots and cries from the wounded, but finally there was an end to hostilities.

Returning the yashmak and djellabah that had not been needed, I thanked our hostess and eased Johannus into the street.

Bodies everywhere! Some of the wounded could be saved. I tore off pieces of my dress and made tourniquets for some. But there was no way I could help

so many people whose blood was ebbing away.

When there was no more material left to tear from my dress without the hem reaching my swollen belly, I prayed for a few of the dying and dead, and turned my attention back to Johannus.

I'd been trying to hide the horrific scene from him, without success. He'd insisted on standing like a foal near its mare.

He was crying very loudly. I felt helpless to stop his tears. Finally, I took a stance in the center of the street just as a UN truck arrived primed with soldiers in neat uniforms and sporting the famous sky-blue berets. The truck stopped for me. Its driver had been at Baku's that special day when Ray arrived with the UN forces to jettison me away from Baku's lair.

He invited Johannus and me into the front cab. Now Johannus perked up: he *loved* riding in a truck, particularly when the driver gave him a Hershey bar, a chocolate candy he'd never tasted before.

We didn't ride far. Before five minutes passed we came nose to nose with Blink-Blink's Mercedes.

Ray jumped out of it to help me climb from the cab. Johannus looked peevish: he'd have liked to drive longer in that great machine.

Suddenly, from what seemed nowhere, Baku's helicopter zoomed down over the Mercedes. Incredibly, Baku opened fire on the car, blasting away at Blink-Blink, who'd asked him for help! But a resistance fighter from the refugees' group appeared, held a flamethrower to his shoulder, and sent a stream of fire to down the helicopter. We saw it explode in flames, and heard a bark that sounded like Baku screaming as it hit the ground.

Blink-Blink had survived, his Santa Claus body intact. It was Baku who had perished.

It was horrible passing so many dead and dying people to reach Blink-Blink's office. There were a few medics doing what little they could for the wounded, but it was like sailors trying to empty the rising water from a leaking ship.

Blink-Blink's office was intact. He pressed me again for my phone, and again he was able to squeeze out one last message. "We need more UN troops to stabilize our situation," he barked.

Pale squawking came out of my phone from the other end.

To me, he said: "You've been lucky, Lovely Ella. Most of my crew are dead. And more Janjaweed are coming from Khartoum. We've only had a reprieve."

"Oh, no!"

"Your Brave Ray wants to get you out of here. And under the present circumstances there's damned all he can do to stop polio. Our hospitals will be full, and what medical supplies weren't destroyed in the mortar fire will be needed for the wounded."

Ray braided his arms around me. "You've done enough here," he said. "I've arranged for us to fly to South Africa. We'll be married there. Yes, and Johannus will be coming too."

CHAPTER 11

Cape Town lies at the base of an extraordinary mountain that's flat on top. The sparkling sea rims the city. There are great beaches.Johannus learned to swim, and I went into the water too in spite of my huge belly.

How had Ray arranged things to leave El Caze and end his job with the Evangelical Mission?

Because he's my Miracle Man. Apparently he'd faced down the top men before going to El Caze. He'd promised to stay put *there* as long as he could be of use, but that would be that.

He'd kept his secret well. I hadn't a clue. He didn't want to have to disappoint me about an early wedding if the polio scare grew into a terrible epidemic that would demand all his care.

When the Janjaweed invaded El Caze and brought the destruction and horrific misery for which they are famous, Ray had his excuse to get out of the remaining months of his contract. There was no way after the Janajaweed destruction that Ray could have continued vaccinating in El Caze against polio.

The tickets to Cape Town had been booked early.

On our arrival there, a comfortable rooming house had been found. No wonder we needed a swim after all the complicated changing of planes and airports that we'd needed after being transported from El Caze to Iriba in Chad,and from there made those connections.

Johannus had loved flying in an airplane. He had been invited up front by pilots in two of the aircraft we took. More importantly, he was ecstatic about the endless meals at our Cape Town rooming house. Oh! How soon he became a gourmet eater instead of just a glutton. He would even bypass plattershe considered had food that was not up to his standard.

Our wedding preparations were simple. We decided to have the ceremony at St.Mary's Church, with a reception after at the Mount Nelson Hotel, nicknamed by most South Africans who spoke English as well as Afrikaans, 'The Nellie.'

Ray wanted to invite his brother and sister to our wedding: I had no relations left who would have come.

But I had traumatic fears that his brother and sister would treat me like a whore who'd captured their brother by getting herself pregnant. Wasn't getting pregnant the best-known trick for a girl who wanted to get married?

Yes, I'd been impressed by the way his brother had handled the all-important telephone conversation with that arrogant flunkey at the British Consulate in Khartoum. That didn't guarantee that he'd overlook the getting-pregnant ploy!

Ray's brother, Ian Bruce, and his sister Fiona flew from Edinburgh, bringing with them one of Ray's orphans who'd excelled at school and won the trip. Both Ian and Fiona went beyond the rules of etiquette to be nice to me. There were no snide insinuations that I'd played the whore to get pregnant to capture their brother. Instead, they quoted to me some very nice things the five orphans had told them about how I'd cared for the boys during our terrible times in the Sudan and Chad.

Looking jolly, his cavalry-officer's moustache dancing, Ian repeated: "Wozeira Ella, she lady be good."

Ian was Ray's best man. Fiona served as Matron of Honor.Johannus was ring boy. Ray's orphan distributed the wedding leaflets to our few guests: a few staff members from Ray's new hospital, and a secretary from the Commonwealth Office I'd met on the beach.

Because it was almost Christmas, both the church and the hotel were magnificently decorated with greenery and fairy lights. There was a Nativity scene at the church, and a huge tree covered with velvet bows topping glass balls in the shape of fruits. But it was South Africa's summer, so there was almost a beachtime atmosphere on the streets, with tourists wearing shorts and T-shirts.

Our wedding party contrasted lyricaly. Ladies wore huge hats and flowing chiffons. Top hats and morning suits were the kit for the men.

Christmas carols were heard everywhere, in the chapel and in the halls of 'The Nellie."

No T-shirts and shorts in the dignified 'Nellie.' Tourists, yes. Sloppy clothes, no. There, a certain oldtime conservatism reigned in its halls filled with well-dressed jacket-and-tie men escorting women in chic Paris creations. No question but they enjoyed its fabled dining room with its unbeatable views.

Our wedding reception was a brief one, because being heavily pregnant I needed to cut it short and return to my bed in our suite.

But I'm afraid that Ray and I celebrated later in a naughty way enjoying our wedding suite with wonderful sex in its king-size bed, and our lovemaking brought on birth pangs. My water broke. I did the suggested deep breathing, and when that didn't work, I asked Ray to call for an ambulance.

Ray had been posted to a fine new hospital in Cape Town with a three year contract, but I wasn't lucky enough to get to go to his hospital.

I went where the ambulance took me. A grim old pre-World War II clinic, with the sovereign's name and a DIEU ET MON DROIT-lettered crest still on it.

This clinic had nurses who still wore regulation caps in the style of hospitals where they had graduated. How did I have time to notice all those nitty-gritties? I went into a very long labor. That's how!

Our little daughter was born twenty hours later. It wasn't an easy birth, but when I saw the delight in Ray's eyes and the wonder in Johannus's eyes, I forgot the birth pangs. I felt even better when I watched our family's glutton, Johannus, giving Hope her first bottle feeding!

We had her baptized Hope. Because she was Africa-born and we believed there was great hope for Africa.

CHAPTER 12

Exactly one year later, having decided to spend Christmas with my friends among the Belgian nuns at El Caze in Darfur, Ray and I returned to our former haunt. We left Hope and Johannus with new friends in Johannusberg.

"Is the city named after me?" Johannus had asked. "Or was *I* named after the city?"

"Neither," I'd replied, taking away a Mars bar from him, because his teeth were beginning to have cavities from too many sweets. "You were named for the Ethiopian Emperor Johannus, or so I was told when I was so lucky as to find you. He was a great emperor."

"Empeeror! Golly, lucky name it is?"!

"He kept out an invading army under Napier that had arrived to conquer Ethiopia and add it to the British Empire. Emperor Johannus raised an army of one hundred thousand warriors, and bested Napier. Our British Museum was even obliged to return an earlier Ethiopian emperor's crown to Johannus."

That story shut up my Johannus. He went off to Johannusberg without a whimper.

What helped, of course, was that a huge basket of foodstuffs went with him as a gift to my friends.

Our baby, Hope, stayed in South Africa with *my friend from the Commonwealth office. That friend, who had lost her job due to running home every few hours to check on HER baby, who was the same age as Hope. She'd said to me: "Just as easy to look* after two as one." I hadn't wanted to expose Hope to El Caze's filth and lack of fresh food.

It was heart-wrenching to leave Hope behind, but it was just as well because El Caze looked no cleaner nor prosperous when we returned than it had a year earlier.

The houses that had been hit by mortars were still in ruins. Trees that had been smashed had not been replaced by young saplings. Plastic shower curtains served as roofs for many refugees who couldn't afford or find a tent. In spite of my campaign against their presence, the gangs of hyenas still nibbled at corpses. Awful!

Blink-Blink had left the camp. He'd returned to Newcastle shortly after Baku's death. Would he get a peerage? Maybe.

One place that showed improvement was the Belgian nuns' compound. They'd had built a clinic made of solid bricks. "Bricks brought to us from Chad in trucks belonging to the United Nations," Sister Aurelie told me merrily. This nun had done well here after replacing Sister Agnes. She had a fresh approach to the horrors of El Caze, feeling optimistic and happy with what little improvements had been made. "And there were enough blocks left over to build a one-room schoolhouse.*And* a chapel. Now, if the rains finally come, we'll be nice and dry in proper buildings." She didn't complainn that the roofs were oftin that might not withstand heavy rains.

And the rains *did* come. I'd never seen El Caze in the rain. Torrents, sheets, blinding blankets of rain took over El Caze.

Two days after our arrival we couldn't think of anything else. We got soaked. Our canvas suitcases couldn't protect our clothes. We'd brought only one pair of shoes each, and had no replacements when those got loose soles.

The nuns were all right for shoes. There had been an order from the mother house in Brussels changing their outfits and a directive even suggesting they show their hair. No more cwimples. No more religious habits. No more disciples'-like open sandals. They'd been sent uniforms resembling what hospital volunteers wear. Very plain, but knee-length.

Their haircuts were in the style of the 1920s flappers' and quite becoming. What a change!

But one elderly nun balked at the change and sat in chapel stolidly wearing the old-fashioned floorlength habit and a wimple to hide her hair. Oh, well! I guess it takes all sorts to fill the world.

And that elderly nun was one sort.

We weren't in a 'proper building.' No, I was housed in a utility tent much like that one I'd shared with poor Bertha.

Ray was barracked in with visiting UN officers. I hate to think it, but perhaps the nuns wouldn't let me share a tent with my husband for fear they'd hear us making love. And they *would* have!

I'd brought an assortment of gifts for my nun friends. Food, of course. Fresh fruits and meat. No fish, I'd been afraid fish would go rotten without a refrigerator. There were pajamas for their orphans, because when on occasion I'd said their bedtime prayers with them, I'd noticed they'd gone to sleep in the rags they'd worn in the daytime..

Ray's gifts were even more varied. For their clinic he'd bought, at discount hypodermic, needles to provide vaccinations and all the paraphernalia needed for medical emergencies that they could handle

For their comfort and safety he'd acquired a dynamo providing spurts of electricity: it worked for four hours alternatively, giving light in the dark hours but during daytimes affording electricity for cooking. As a bonus the dynamo's electricity fed a vacuum cleaner that gobbled the ever-present dust.

For us, Sister Aurelie had sneaked from the kitchen a bowl of porridge, just as Sister Agnes would have done Could I ever forget how she'd invited me to share the Quaker Oats sent her by her family, and how she'd dug in the dust for scattered grains when our handfuls were sent to the ground by desperately starving children.

Dust was still an enemy in Darfur, even with so much rain!

Not overwhelming outdoors though, now that the rains had come. An unhealthy menace indoors, housing fleas.

Tracking our way in the alleys' mud, we'd eventually found the spot where Malaku had stepped between me and a fatal bullet. I'd had made a copper plaque with Malaku's name and the date he died. After a short prayer, Ray and I had it installed on the spot.

I'd brought a living azalea to plant at Lloyd's burial plot.

All was *not* gloomy! Particularly at the Belgian nuns' compound.It being Christmastime we'd brought strings of coloured baubles and tinsel for a miniature plastic evergreen tree. The nuns installed it in the chapel along with a group of plaster nativity statues sent to one of them by her family in Belgium. With the dynamo working, the trees'lights glowed during Mass.

But what is Christmas without surprise gifts? Not all of them utilitarian!

For the nuns I distributed sugar-coated almonds. For the children, toys. The girls got tiny dolls. The boys:miniature trucks. All exactly alike so there'd be no squabbling.

Our last morning at El Caze fell on Boxing Day.

Ray said plaintively: "I think you should take something to that hospital where you worked. No happy memories, I know. But, those people have had it very hard."

"You *would* say that."

"Terrible, what happened with that hospital. All the promises made by government agencies were just that. Promises. Promises, promises. I looked in there day before yesterday to ask if I could help in any way, No, thank you. I was practically told 'Get Out' as if I was some kind of snoop."

"But, in a way you were."

"So! I could maybe have leaned on some government officials to suggest improvements. I was told 'government will rebuild and give us a new hospital, no point trying to fix up this one.' God, there was still a large hole where a missile hit it in last year's fighting. It could be ten years or more before Khartoum does ANYTHING."

"Wards still filthy?"

"Filthy, germ-ridden. Be better for some patients not to be sent there. Die of the flesh-eating bug."

"Any Christmas decorations for the Christian patients?"

"You must be kidding! Most of the beds don't even have sheets. Patients are on bare mattresses."

"I'll take some food to the volunteers. Oh! When I remember how hungry I was when I worked there, and how much it meant to me that a patient's family gave me some maniac."

"We haven't much left to give away."

"Buy some local produce?"

"Could do."

"Let's."

We spent our final morning in Darfur, grubbing around in what passes for a marketplace at El Caze. It's nothing more than a collection of tents where the tradesmen live with their families but sell whatever they can get.

I didn't call on the new Director to say goodbye. Nor did I go to meet the Administrator who'd followed on after Blink-Blink. Not after witnessing the disgusting condition of our one lone hospital.

The UN truck that took us to the nearest airport duly swept past Baku's compound. An immense amount of activity had taken over every area. There were two competing hotels already open on the site of his "collection," with a heliport near where his lone helicopter had been parked. His house remained, now used for the executives overseeing all that construction.It looked unaltered but had even more luxurious planting around it. A new addition was a formal Versailles-type garden that had been built around fountains in this *arid* place. What a waste of the pitiful supply of water!It couldn't be very pleasant to stay in either of those hotels without water. Imagine not being able to flush!

Our truck passed the McFees' village. No sign of life there. It looked like the villagers had all abandoned their homes after the polio epidemic had devastated the place. Like townspeople who'd fled from a medieval plague, they'd moved away.McFEE'S OWN HOME HAD BEEN BURNED DOWN. WHY? AS A TORCH IN MEMORY OF HIS WIFE?OR BY JANJAWEED, to instill more fear!

Goodbye Darfur. We'd tried, but hadn't been able to give any effective help. We'd wanted to stop current plagues. We'd wanted to improve the environment, bring its people clean water and help plant trees where there were no longer any. We'd wanted to give a home to orphans that in other cultures would have been aborted.

Hello, Cape Town.Time now to collect our own little baby Hope from my Commonwealth friend, and send for Johannus. To use an expression from JOELY'S DIARY: *bliss*!